Ridden Hard Put Up Wet

AN ANTHOLOGY OF SHORT STORIES
BY
FREDRICK W. BOLING

Copyright © 2000-2001 by Fredrick W. Boling

ISBN 0-9722808-2-0

Published by:

BIGHORN PUBLISHING

35 La Canada Way
Hot Springs Village, AR 71909

Cover designed by Martin Gruelle.

Printed in the United States of America

For Taylor Fogarty
who first published most of
these stories in American Western Magazine.

Contents

The Resurrection of Butch Slade   9

Doc Ruby's Secret   15

Jake Tillie's Last Dance   24

Doctor Magic's Medicine Wagon   32

A Tough Bounty Hunter   40

Sam Grace's Infernal Machine   50

Buffalo Bill, Chung Lee and Me   65

Bill Pickett and Friend   82

Who Shot Count Rudolph Jäger?   93

Fabian Fagan's Folly   110

A Sailing T Ranch Feliz Navidad   138

Headin' For The Last Roundup   145

The Resurrection Of Butch Slade

The main thing I remember about Butch Slade was the grin plastered on the face of his corpse. I don't suppose anyone thought anything about it, because that's how he always looked: bloodshot eyes and tobacco-stained teeth bared between those lips screwed up at the corners. Now that he was dead and laid out in a pine box in front of Pa's furniture store, everyone came to look at him. Come to think of it, I don't reckon he'd of minded.

I was only ten at the time. My Pa had the only furniture store in Lander, Wyoming. Besides bedsteads and tables, he sold caskets. That's kind of the way they did things back then. A hundred dollars would buy you a fancy hardwood casket stained and varnished like your parlor table. He didn't sell many of those. Most folks went for the twenty-five-dollar pine box with the nailed-down lid. It didn't seem to matter. None of his customers ever bragged or complained about their accommodations.

Pa didn't intend to bury Butch in the pine box he was laid out in. It was just for show. And it was a good place to keep him until the ground thawed. Sometimes that was as late as March or even April in the Wind River Mountains. He was going to bury him in *the buff*. That's what Pa called taking a gunslinger's corpse out to Boot Hill on a buckboard and planting him dressed in the duds he had on when he died. Well, that's what Pa intended for Butch, but he never got the chance. Butch disappeared right in broad daylight, pine box and all. Pa was beside himself, not because Butch came up missing, but losing a twenty-five dollar casket sent him into a cussing fit.

Butch showed up right after the first snow dusted the main drag. He stepped out of the stagecoach wearing nothing but black—black hat, parka, shirt, pants, and boots. All were black, even the cartridge belt, holster and grips on his Colt .45. And come to think of it, his hair, eyebrows, and mustache were black as the bottom of Ma's kettle that she boiled Pa's starched shirts in. But it was the grin he was wearing like he'd ridden too long facing a blizzard that made me want to get a closer look at him.

"Hey kid," he yelled as I peeked around the corner of Pa's store. "Come here."

I jerked my head back, hoping he'd just go on about his business. No telling what he had in mind, and I sure didn't want anything to do with his kind. Ma always told me not to talk to strangers. And Butch Slade was strange, that was for certain.

"Hey kid," he said, stepping around the corner toward me.

I reckon my heart nearly stopped as I stared at his mean eyes. I wanted to run, but fear had cemented my feet to the frozen alleyway. "Ye... yes... sir," I stammered.

"Reckon y'live here?" he said around the cigarette dangling from the corner of his mouth.

"Over there," I said, pointing at our house across the street.

He glanced at our place, and then pulled back his parka. I'll never forget that Colt .45 with its big black grips shinning like one of Pa's ebony caskets. He patted his holster a couple of times and sort of shoved it a mite lower on his hip. "I'm looking for an old friend," he said, eyeing me real hard.

"Yes, sir," I said and began to back away a couple of steps.

"Ain't no need t'be scared," he said, trying to sound more friendly. "I don't shoot kids."

"Yes, sir."

"I'm looking for Will Dawson," he said and puffed a couple of drags on his cigarette. "Y'know him?"

Everybody in Lander knew Will Dawson. Will had come to Lander after he was released from the penitentiary at Laramie. That was before I was born. Nobody talked much about Will's life before he went to prison. Just why he went to prison, I wasn't real certain, but my pa said that it had something to do with blowing up a safe on a Union Pacific train. The explosion and Wyoming winds scattered greenbacks all over Uinta County, but the train robbers got away with all the gold. Maybe Will didn't have anything to do with the robbery, but it was rumored that he started our only bank in Lander with several canvas bags filled with gold. "Reckon he's over there at the bank," I said, turning away to high tail it for the store.

After I got in Pa's store, I watched Butch walking toward the bank. "Quit gawking out that window, Thomas Geiger," Pa yelled from the back of the store where he was building a new oak casket. "I need you to help me varnish this coffin."

"Who's it for?" I asked, dipping my brush into the can of varnish.

"Don't rightly know," he said. "I got a cashier's check and an unsigned order for an oak coffin in the mail last week."

That casket sat in the back of the store for a couple of months waiting for whoever sent Pa a hundred dollars. It was a real beauty as far as caskets go. Whoever ordered it wanted a genuine "customized case," as Pa called the fancy coffins. According to the order's instructions, Ma covered the bottom with horsehair padding and lined it with shiny red satin. Three brass handles for pallbearers to tote the thing hung from each side. That many handles meant that its occupant had to have at least six friends, which wasn't too common in our rowdy town at that time.

Butch Slade moved into Aunt Jane's boarding house up the road on the north side of town. He walked everywhere he went. I couldn't figure why he didn't buy himself a horse or even a buckboard if he didn't take to pounding leather with his rear. But he didn't seem to mind the daily stroll he took down the center of the road to the Watering Hole Saloon next door to the bank. That's when things began to happen.

Butch's bent for poker was insatiable, as was his taste for whiskey and the *soiled doves* that plied their trade upstairs above the saloon. He seemed to have plenty of money to pursue all three.

The first incident happened on a Saturday night. Pa had whipped me once for gawking through the saloon's window at the goings on inside. So, it took a lot of thinking about that razor strap before I decided to satisfy my curiosity bone that had been itching for weeks. It was just past dark when I snuck across the street and crouched down under the window. They were having a rip-roaring time inside. The piano keys were being hammered, and the bottles and glasses were clanking, and the bar maids were laughing. How I wished I were old enough to go inside without answering to my pa.

I don't recall how long I squatted there, aching to take a peek, but scared of getting caught was hard to overcome. Well, I finally decided I had to look before my legs busted right in two. I eased my head up until my eyes peered over the windowsill. My heart jumped right up in my throat at what I saw. One of the barmaids was up on the bar, dancing and slinging her skirt clear over her head. A crowd of men was bellied up around the bar a whooping and clapping something fierce. The more they clapped and whistled the harder she danced. I was so rapt at what was going on that I didn't hear any sounds of the lowlife backshooter slipping up behind me. And then the biggest bang I'd ever heard roared above my head.

I got back to our porch before I turned around to see what was going on. There stood Will Dawson right where I'd been squatting. He was aiming a big hogleg through the window he had just blown to smithereens. I didn't get to see the finish because Pa's big hand grabbed me by the seat of my pants and yanked me into the house.

"You get in your room," Pa yelled, picking up the keys to the store. "I'll tend to you when I get back."

As it turned out, Will Dawson bit the dust that night. He had tried to shoot Butch who was playing poker with his back to the window I was peeking through. Well, Will missed Butch and killed Doc Mosley sitting across the table from Butch. Butch was fast with that .45 of his; I'd say faster than an alley cat with turpentine on his caboose. Before Will could get off another shot, Butch shot him dead.

That's when we found out who had ordered the oak

casket.   After the corpses were carried over to our store, Butch walked in to pay his last respects.   Pa got real nervous when Butch began to ransack Doc's pockets.   He was afraid Butch wouldn't leave enough of the deceased's winnings for at least a twenty-five-dollar pine box.   When all of Doc's pockets had been emptied, Butch counted all of the green backs and gold double-eagles.   And then he counted an equal amount of poker chips and slipped them into Doc's pocket.   "Here's twenty-five to bury Doc proper," he said to Pa.   "And that oak casket I sent you a hundred to build is for my friend, Will Dawson."

"Damned sorry friend," Pa said after Butch walked back to the saloon.   "Can't figure why Will tried to back-shoot Butch, but, what's more, I can't believe Will was such a piss-poor shot."

The next morning, Butch walked into the bank and plopped his butt down in Will's leather chair.   He leaned back, propped his big black boots on Will's desk, rolled a Bull Durham cigarette and settled down for a quiet smoke.

When Angie Dawson, that's Will's widow, walked in to take over the bank, Butch just sat there with that silly grin kicking up the ends of his Earp mustache.   Angie stopped smack dab in front of Will's desk and grabbed Butch by his boots.   "Get out of here," she screamed and shoved his boots off Will's desk.

"You get out," Butch drawled, real calm like.   "This is my bank, Mrs. Dawson."

"Your bank?" she yelled and she could really yell.   "I'm Will's heir, not you."

Butch pulled a document out of his inside pocket and slammed it on the desk.   "Oh, no you ain't—read this."

She did, and that's when all hell broke loose.   It seems that Will, Butch and three other members of their gang had pulled off the Union Pacific job.   During their getaway, Will disappeared with all of the gold.   The railroad detectives caught him but not until he had squirreled away the loot.   Butch and the others hid out for quite a spell while Will did the time.   Now you see why Butch ordered the casket and came to Lander to even the score with Will.

Well—now for the rub.   Butch hadn't given Angie the proper respect.   When she read that document, which was Will's

Last Will and Testament, she got real steamed. Butch had made Will sign every bit of his earthly goods over to him in the event of his death. Of course, Will hadn't planned on going to Boot Hill before Butch, so it didn't require a lot of persuading on Butch's part. Without hesitating, she reached down where her bosoms peeked above her blouse and yanked out one of those Derringer pistols. It was a double shot model, and both bullets sealed Butch's grin for good.

She panicked and ran out the back door before anybody came and found what she had done. Everybody figured she killed Butch, but the marshal was sort of sweet on her, so Pa said. That's why he waited a couple of days before riding out to Will's place to arrest her.

She skipped out on an early stage the morning after Butch came up missing. I reckon she didn't want to be a banker after all, because she took all the gold out of the safe before she left. But before she skedaddled, she paid a couple of town drunks to swipe Butch's corpse and Pa's pine box and tote them over to the bank. That's where they found Butch along with *Will Dawson's Last Will and Testament.* Both of them were locked up in the vault behind Will's high-backed leather chair.

Pa got the same town drunks to tote Butch and his pine box back to the funeral parlor. That's when he found a penciled note and a sealed envelope in a pocket of Butch's black leather vest. Angie had addressed them to Rudolf Geiger, that's my pa, knowing he would be the one who would find them. Pa read out loud the sentiments Angie expressed in her note. "To whomever might be concerned about the death of Butch Slade. I killed him. He's a lowdown-murdering thief. I'm praying that old Satan will claim his moldering carcass if it ever gets resurrected."

Then Pa opened the envelope and pulled out a wad of green backs. He waved that fistful of dollars over his head and yelled, "Whoopee! I'm buildin' Butch another oak coffin just like the one he bought for Will. He deserves it—yes sir—he surely does."

Doc Ruby's Secret

The main things I remember about Doc Ruby were his breath, his stethoscope, and the big hogleg that he wore jammed behind his belt.

The common comment around Lander, Wyoming, that's where I got born, was that Doc could raise up a dead man by just blowing in his face. It wasn't that his breath was bad—it was powerful bad. You see, for one thing he ate a lot of smelly Limburger cheese smeared on soda crackers. And then there was the medicinal brandy that he chased it down with. I suppose the main reason he ate that kind of stuff was because he didn't have a wife to straighten him out. At least that's what Ma said.

Then there was the fancy stethoscope he carried in a little black bag. That shiny thing was cold as a dead man's face. I ought to know, because I'd come in contact with both of them—the dead man in Pa's funeral parlor and Doc's stethoscope when I got the measles.

That brings me to Doc's big hogleg. It was a nickel-plated Remington .44 with an extra long barrel. He always carried it jammed behind his belt buckle no matter where he went, even during funerals. By the way, that's the only time Doc ever stepped inside a church house.

Doc Ruby came to our town a couple of months after Will Dawson's lousy aim kilt Doc Mosley over at the Watering Hole Saloon. I'll never forget the day he drove his buggy with slick, patent leather fenders into Lander behind a big chestnut gelding. Gosh-a'-mighty, but Doc was sitting tall in that rubber-tired Studebaker buggy. The crown of his "Sugar Loaf" Stetson nearly touched the roof of the buggy's canvas top.

When Doc whoa'd to a stop in front of Pa's store, I had my nose plastered against the window gawking at that buggy, because I'd never seen one like it before. Doc stepped out of his buggy and started to straighten up. His lanky carcass sort of unfolded and got taller and taller just like a picture of Abe Lincoln I'd seen in one of Ma's *Harper's* magazines. He was wearing one of those long, frock coats that were all splotched with alkali road dust. "Where's your pa?" he yelled at me, tying his horse to our hitching rail.

"He's out at Boot Hill," I said, pulling my nose away from the windowpane.

Doc's size fourteen boots clopped across the board sidewalk and into our store. He knuckled his big, reddish-brown mustache and walked on back toward Pa's funeral parlor. "How about your ma?" he said without looking back at me.

"I'll get her," I said, trailing along behind him.

That's when he stopped and turned around. "You mean she ain't here—who's minding the store?"

"Me," I said, pushing out my chest like Polly Boy. He was Aunt Jane's red and blue macaw that she kept in a cage in the parlor of her boarding house. He had a real foul mouth and would say some of the most shocking things to folks when they came in the front door. Most of the lady folks in town refused to have tea at her place because of his obscene outbursts. Aunt Jane tried covering his cage with a sheet, but it didn't help. That smelly old bird just kept on cussing and yelling 'cause he wanted to see out.

Doc reached into his pocket for pinch-nosed spectacles that he always put on when he wanted to see real well. He perched them on the end of his nose and bent down to stare at my shaking composure. "You can't be no more than nine," he said, eyeing me with those bloodshot eyes of his.

"No sir," I croaked, "I'm ten."

"Ten!" he said, straightening up. "You aint many days past ten. Go fetch your ma."

I did, and she went over to the store to see what Doc wanted. As it turned out, Pa had sent a letter to the medical school in Denver asking for a new Doc to replace the one he'd planted out on Boot Hill. Everybody thought Doc Ruby was who they sent, but... reckon I'd better hold up on telling that so as not to get ahead of my story.

Doc got room and board up at Aunt Jane's place and hung up his shingle outside Doc Mosley's old office upstairs above the drugstore. Well, it really wasn't a drugstore like we know today. First, Doc Mosley had peddled patent medicines and booze out of his store, and then Doc Ruby just carried on the same after he took it over. I reckon he sold more laudanum and whiskey than anything else. Of course, his concocted potions for the women folks sold real well, too.

It wasn't long afterwards that I came down with the big red measles. Ma used up all of her remedies, most of which were worse than my disease, during the first couple of days after I took to my bed. She didn't know what I had until Pa finally insisted on having Doc Ruby look me over. I can still see him as he sat down next to my cot of misery. He set his little black bag between number fourteen boots and flipped it open. That's when I got introduced to being close to Doc's beard, his Limburger breath, and the cold steel of his stethoscope. "Quit your squirming," he said, trying to keep up with my evasive ways.

I tried but the stench of his breath and the tickle of his beard against my bare chest kept after me. My high fever warmed up his stethoscope right away, so I didn't mind it anymore. No matter how hard I tried, I just couldn't face the fetid breeze blowing out of his nostrils. That's when Ma got into one of her twits when I finally said, "Phewee," and pulled the pillow over my face.

"Now you straighten up," she said, jerking the pillow away. "Doctor Ruby is trying to help you."

"He's all right," Doc said, pulling my eyelids apart and then he asked Ma for a spoon. He slithered the handle of the spoon into my mouth and got down real close while Ma held the lamp so he could see. While I was trying to keep from breathing so I wouldn't catch his stinky breath, he kept repeating, "Hum— Ah—Ha."

Those utterings seemed to set Ma to worrying. "What's he got, Doctor Ruby?" she said, with her eyes getting real wide, sort of like the time Pa came home drunk.

Doc patted her on the hand and turned his attention to

her instead of me, for which I was grateful. "Now, Mrs. Geiger," he droned, "your youngster is just coming down with the measles. I'll have him up and about in a couple of weeks."

"Measles?" she said, looking like what Doc said wasn't so. "Where did he get the measles?"

He assured Ma that catching the measles wasn't like getting a social disease, which he spelled out in terms that she caught right onto, but I didn't. Like he said, a couple of weeks and an assortment of his pills and elixirs found me recovered.

Doc got real busy calling on about every home in and around Lander because the measles really took off at that time. Some said he brought the affliction with him in his little black bag just so he could get a lot of business. In fact, Ma was the one who came up with that idea after every kid in town got sick. And it didn't take long for Doc to hear the rumor she had started. That's when he came calling.

I was sitting by the window in Ma's rocking chair sipping broth when I spied Doc coming down the stairway on the side of the drugstore. His number fourteens carried him straight toward our house. He had a big book under his arm and a scowl on his face as he stamped up the steps of our front porch. He slammed his big fist against the door facing so hard it rattled Pa's portrait of old Abe Lincoln hanging over the mantle. "Mrs. Geiger," he bellowed. Yes indeed, he bellowed just like the ringmaster at a circus Pa took me to in Denver once.

I heard Ma slamming pots and pans away in the kitchen, that's because she didn't want anybody seeing clutter in her house. Doc knocked again, even louder than the first time, and hollered loud enough to bring Aunt Jane out on her front porch to see what was going on. Ma scampered through the parlor drying her hands on that big calico apron of hers. "Just a minute," she screeched, and then tripped over Pa's footstool. The whole house shuddered as she plopped down right in the middle of the parlor. I'll say one thing for Doc; he didn't wait for an invitation. He came right in and helped Ma up onto the sofa.

After Ma composed herself and assured Doc she wasn't hurt, he flipped open his big book and laid it in her lap. "Now,

Mrs. Geiger," he said, trying to sound calm. But I could see in his eyes that he was madder than a hive of bees chasing a bear with his snout full of their honey. "I want you to read what Doctor William Osler has to say about the epidemiology of measles."

Ma looked at Doc with her big brown eyes, which were the prettiest eyes in Lander, according to Pa, and let loose her wiles on that poor man. "Oh, Doctor Ruby," she said real breathy just like one of the gals over at the Watering Hole Saloon. "Whatever do you mean?"

He pointed his finger at the intended writing of the good Doctor Osler. "Mrs. Geiger, measles doesn't get carried around in a doctor's bag. If you'll read this, you'll see that it is a contagion spread from an infected person to another person."

"Oh, Doctor Ruby," she said, trying to lift up that heavy book so she could read it. "You are so smart."

I could tell by Doc's face that Ma's sweet-talk was finding a home in his soul. He just sat there with a grin betwixt his mustache and beard as Ma read while tracing each word with her finger.

Her crowning comment sent Doc away a happy man. "Oh, my, Doctor Ruby," she said, handing him his book. "You must give a talk at the guild's next meeting and explain all of this to the ladies."

I can still hear him whistling as he walked across the street toward the saloon to buy drinks for the house. But Doc's glory was soon squelched by what happened next.

Aunt Jane's talking macaw had been the constant companion of an old sea captain for a lot of years. You see, that ancient bird had visited just about every port from Shanghai to London perched on the shoulder of that foul-mouthed old salt. Well, it seems that during one of those voyages Doc Ruby happened to have signed on as the ship's surgeon. He was fresh out of medical school and had a lust in his heart to see the world before settling down. Several years later, the old captain died and left all of his earthly goods to his only surviving relative. That's how Aunt Jane got all of her brother's possessions, which included his blabber-mouthed macaw named Polly Boy.

The first incident between Polly Boy and Doc Ruby happened the morning after Doc moved into Aunt Jane's boarding house. But it wasn't told around town until about six months later. That's when Ma wheedled it and some other titillating stuff out of Miss Elberta Lightfoot. Miss Lightfoot had been living at Aunt Jane's place for longer than I could remember. She was an old maid that ran our one-roomed schoolhouse with a switch in one hand and a bell in the other. She spilt the story one day while shopping at Halley's General Store. Miss Lightfoot and Ma had one crowning fault that kept our town in a tizzy most of the time. They were gossips with no peers. They knew everything that happened, no matter where, even before Mr. Rhodes at *The Lander Bugle* got wind of it. If you wanted to get the lowdown on somebody or something, you just asked Ma or Miss Lightfoot.

When Ma came back from the store that day, she had a shine in her eyes that was there whenever she heard some real exciting gossip. News has to be shared, she always said, or it'll just wither away. And Ma wasn't one to hide a good piece of news. "Mister Geiger," she bellowed, coming through the doorway carrying a sack filled with stuff she'd bought. I never heard her call my pa Rudolf, which was his given name, except when she was sweet-talking him. It was always, Mister Geiger. "Pa ain't home," I said.

"Oh, dear me," she muttered, bustling through the parlor.

I knew what she wanted me to say. "What's the matter, Ma?"

The next thing I knew, she came back into the parlor with a grin playing all across her face. "Oh, I wish your pa was here, I've just heard the most awful thing about Doctor Ruby and…."

I could tell she wanted to spill what she had heard, but I reckon she thought my ears were too tender for such sordid things. Several times she started to say something, but she'd stop and wring her hands. "Oh—where is your pa?" she finally said, looking out the parlor window.

"Doc Ruby came by while you were at the store and asked Pa to go with him."

Ma gasped, clamped her hand across her mouth, and then dropped it to speak. "He did? Where on earth did they go?"

"Up to Aunt Jane's."

"Why?"

"He didn't say."

That's when Ma plopped her bag of stuff on the floor and busted into a fit of weeping and wailing. It took a lot of my comforting words and back patting before she settled down.

When Pa got home, Ma was waiting for him in their bedroom away from my delicate ears. At first I couldn't hear anything, just Ma crying like a cat with its tail caught under a rocking chair. Pa kept trying to get her to stop and tell him what was the matter. Well, after she had gotten Pa's full and undivided attention, she laid it out for him. She was speaking real low and I couldn't make out what she was saying for certain, but from Pa's reaction, I'd say it was pretty bad. "What?" he yelled loud enough to be heard clear out on the street.

Ma and Pa didn't talk to one another for about a week after their encounter in the bedroom. I never knew what silence really did to get life out of whack until we got into the middle of that week. It isn't just the not speaking, its the glaring looks and pouty sniffs that will turn the world into an unfit place to live.

I tried to mediate between them the best that a ten-year old could, but all my efforts went barren as an empty bucket. Life sort of got back to normal after Parson Hicks dropped in to find out why we hadn't been to church for two Sundays in a row.

Just when I thought whatever Ma had found out about Doc Ruby had gone into oblivion, the whole thing took off like a pesky cowpoke getting thrown by a bucking bronco. That was the day Doc Ruby pulled out his big .44 and shot Polly Boy right in his cage. They said red and blue feathers filled Aunt Jane's parlor like a whirlwind blowing through a chicken house when that big lead bullet stopped the bird's blabbing for good.

Doc Ruby left town during the night after Polly Boy flew to the heavenly rain forest in the sky. That's when Mr. Rhodes went out to interview Aunt Jane about the whole affair. But you see, she wasn't there, because she had left with Doc.

Some said he made her go with him, but Ma and Miss Lightfoot knew better. According to Miss Lightfoot, Aunt Jane and Doc had hit it off from the start. She also claimed that he wasn't the only man with whom Aunt Jane had been hitting it off. She named several, some of them high-ups, but I'd best not be telling who they were except to say one of them wasn't Pa. She used that tamed-down expression, cohabitation, to soften its impact. But, even I knew what she was talking about. I don't know to this day, how Aunt Jane could stand Doc's breath, but I reckon she didn't mind it as much as I did.

It was too bad that Mr. Rhodes waited so long to follow up on the rumors spread by Ma and Miss Lightfoot. After he interviewed Miss Lightfoot, the whole episode got published in the weekly edition of *The Lander Bugle*.

Mr. Rhodes did a proper job in cutting out the juicy parts that would have offended the weak-at-heart women folks who were married to some of Aunt Jane's visitors. I'll do the best I can to tell you what he printed, not word for word mind you, but it went something like this: Lander is without a doctor once more. Following the unfortunate demise of our beloved Doctor Mosley, Mayor Rudolf Geiger inquired for a replacement with the Denver College of Physician and Surgeons. When Doctor Ruby came to town, we naturally assumed that the folks in Denver had sent him, but that wasn't the case. As it turned out, Doctor Ruby had recently escaped from a Shanghai prison where he had been incarcerated for committing the vilest of crimes on the high seas. During his tenure as the ship's surgeon aboard a British merchant ship, *The Orient Voyage*, Doctor Ruby led a mutinous revolt by the ship's crew. Their motive was the theft of over a ton of gold listed on the ship's inventory. Ruby murdered the first mate and set the ship's master, Captain Belding, adrift in a longboat along with Polly Boy. Purely by good fortune, Captain Belding and Polly Boy were rescued by a British warship after they had drifted in the Pacific for nearly a week.

Captain Belding charged Doc Ruby with murder and mutiny for which Ruby was convicted following his capture in Shanghai. If it hadn't been for the providential meeting between

Doctor Ruby and Polly Boy, we would have never known about Ruby's sordid past. Miss Lightfoot claimed to have overheard Polly Boy's outburst when she arrived home from school the day Doc Ruby moved into Aunt Jane's place. "What did Polly Boy say when he spied Doctor Ruby?" this reporter asked Miss Lightfoot.

"Doc Ruby! Murderer! Quack! Murderer! Quack!" she replied and began to giggle. "But I dare not tell you what he said after Doc Ruby moved into Aunt Jane's room."

Jake Tillie's Last Dance

The main things I remember about Jake Tillie were his high-topped boots, silver-rowel spurs and black sombrero. Those boots came clean up to his knees and had long mule-ear pulls so's he could get them on. Most folks said he didn't need any pulls, because he never took off those fancy-stitched high leathers. And I reckon my pa was of the same mind, because he buried Jake with them still on out on boot hill.

Jake was real proud of those boots. He claimed to have taken them off a Mexican bandito by the name of Juan Martinez down in Juarez just across the Rio Grande from El Paso, Texas. That was after him and Juan got into a shootout over a marked poker deck. I never did hear Jake say which one of them had done the cheating, but that doesn't matter 'cause Juan lost his boots and sombrero.

Jake Tillie fancied himself to be a dancing man. What with Juan's silver-studded "Chihuahua" spurs that jingled like harness bells on a Laplander's reindeer, you could hear his fancy flamingo steps every night.

I'd just turned sixteen the day before Jake rode into Casper, Wyoming astride a bandy-legged cayuse that nobody with any sense would even drop a lariat on. Jake stuck out like a Mexican flag run up over the Alamo with his gold-trimmed sombrero, black leather vest, and striped britches tucked inside high-topped boots.

Pa had moved Ma and me from Lander to Casper during the summer of ninety right after Wyoming got taken into the Union. He bought out Henry Slessinger's furniture store and funeral parlor, because Ma wanted to move to a civilized town. She had showed Pa an article in the *Casper Weekly Mail* that listed the Casper census at 544 living souls. And most ever'body didn't even know that Lander existed.   But her winning argument was our getting coffins and furniture shipped in on the Fremont, Elkhorn and Missouri Valley Railroad, which was bound to turn us a higher profit.

Ma discovered that the move wasn't all that she wanted. It seems that there was about as much uncivilized stuff going on as in Lander, but she said nary a word about moving back. That is, until I started running around with Jake Tillie. Then she got her nose out o' joint when Pa told her to quit fussing, because I was just going through growing pains.

Like I said, Jake came to Casper riding that good-for-nothing horse, which died the day after he tied him to the hitching rail in front of Robert White's Saloon. Reckon it just up and died from neglect, at least that's what the town marshal accused Jake of. Jake just kept on playing poker and drinking booze 'cause there wasn't any law against abusing a horse.

Anyways, that's when I met Jake face-to-face. You see, there wasn't anybody in Casper that did away with dead horses. I'll never forget how livid my pa got when Marshal Tigman walked in and ast him what he'd charge t'drag a dead horse out of town. "Dispose of what?" Pa yelled with his face no more'n six inches from Tigman's eyes that had saucered out like those of a spooked mule.

"Now Mister Geiger," Tigman said, sort of backing away while holding up his hands. "I ain't aiming to insult you by what I ast. It's just that I know you got those two Percheron horses that you pull your glass-sided funeral coach with."

Pa peered at the marshal over his pinch-nosed spectacles. "And you figure they can drag a dead horse?"

"That's about it," Tigman said and tongued his chaw waiting for Pa to reply.

"Who's going' t'pay me?"

"That new hombre by the name of Jake Tillie up at Robert White's Saloon."

"He agree to that?"

The marshal patted the big Colt Peacemaker cradled in his holster. "No, but he will."

Pa scratched his bald noggin while pondering how much

to charge for dragging off a dead horse. Then he turned to me and said, "Run up to the saloon and tell Mister Tillie that he owes me ten dollars for disposing of his horse."

I hadn't ever been inside a saloon before, but I had peeked into one through the window back in Lander. That's when Will Dawson kilt Doc Mosley by mistake. I won't ever forget the odors that slithered up my nose when I walked into White's place. A blend of spilt whiskey, stale cigar smoke, and unwashed armpits nearly shoved me right back out the door.

I recognized Jake Tillie from the big sombrero dangling down his back on the end of a leather thong tied around his neck. He was chomping on an unlit cigar jammed into the corner of his mouth and his eyes were studying his hand of cards. The three cowpokes he was playing with were staring at the big stacks of red, white, and blue chips in front of Tillie. I reckon he was winning more than they figured he ought to.

After they finished their hand and Jake was raking in more winnings, I took off my hat and cleared the jitters out of my throat. Jake glanced at me while he was building another stack of chips. "What are you staring at, kid?"

"Uh, are you Jake Tillie?" I said, fingering the brim o' my hat.

"Yeah," he said, sounding real gruff. "Who wants t'know?"

"My pa sent me."

"Your pa, who's your pa?"

"He's a mortician," I said, trying to sound well bred.

"A what?"

"Mortician, you know, an undertaker."

That's when I heard the jingle of those spurs of his for the first time. He slid back his chair and stood up. "You're interrupting my game, kid," he said, toying with a stack of dollar chips. "What does your pa want of me?"

"Your horse is dead."

He began to chuckle. "I know that—don't tell me your pa wants to bury my horse?"

"No, sir, the marshal wants him to drag it out of town."

"Well, that's fine with me, tell 'im t'go ahead."

"Yes, sir... but."

"But what?"

"His fee... is."

"Fee?"

"Ten dollars."

Jake stared at me with the hardest look I'd ever seen. "If the marshal wants my horse drug off, go get your ten dollars from him."

One of the cowpokes began to laugh, and then pretty soon the whole crowd stopped playing poker and drinking, and filled the saloon with guffaws. Well, Jake didn't take to all that commotion. He filled his hand with a Derringer, which he pulled out of his high-topped boot, and aimed it square between my eyes. "Now, kid," he snarled, "you just sashay your butt out o' here and go give your pa and the marshal my answer."

"Yes, sir," I said and waited to hear his answer.

"Y'can tell 'em that the buzzards will eat my horse right out there in the street before I'll pay anyone ten dollars."

I knew my welcome had thinned out like lard on a hot skillet. I nodded and stepped backwards toward the door. Just then, a hand slapped me on the shoulder. "Hold up there, son," a man said, squeezing my shoulder with a grip strong enough to make a gorilla cringe.

The grip belonged to Mister White, the bartender and owner of the saloon. He quickly pointed out to Jake the errors of his ways while Jake stared up the double muzzles of Mister White's scattergun. Jake booted his Derringer and handed me a ten-dollar gold eagle. "Okay, kid, tell your pa to go ahead."

Ma began to speak to Pa again after she found out that his reputation as a mortician had not been sullied by his disposing of Jake's dead horse. But Pa let Tigman know right off that he'd drug off his last dead horse. So, from that day on, Pa just buried human beings, those succumbing to natural causes and a goodly bunch that didn't.

Having been exposed to the going's on inside White's Saloon sort of changed my life. I had just turned sixteen and I'd run smack dab into a time when I was trying to decide the difference between good times and minding Pa and Ma. Since my days up to that time had been totally devoid of any sinful pursuits, the temptations of gambling, drinking, and enjoying the wiles of pretty gals began to dog me. I finally decided that Jake Tillie seemed to have the right slant on things. He was winning lots of money, which bought him plenty of Havana cheroots and all the whiskey he could drink. But I reckon the most enticing part were the gals.

The first thing I did was to bust open my bank that I'd been stuffing my money into for a lot of years. I went down to Tidwell's Store and bought me a complete new outfit. Of all my new duds, I was most proud of my new boots. They weren't as tall as Jake's, but they'd been polished until they was slick as lizard sweat. And I thought my spurs were even fancier than Jake's. Mine weren't all silvery like his, but they were solid brass with silver rowels, and jingled just like his.

After I put on all my new stuff, Mister Tidwell stuffed all my old duds into a gunnysack and counted out my change, which came to four dollars and twenty-five cents. I ast him to keep my old duds until I came back—my intentions was to try my hand at poker over at the saloon.

Well, Jake Tillie won my four dollars and twenty-five cents on the first hand of five-card stud. When I told him and the other two players that I didn't have any more money, they busted into more hee-haws than I wanted t'hear. Amid all that taunting, I stood up and slung my chair aside. That was a foolish gesture on my part, because Jake took offense before I could set my spurs t'jingling. Jeez, but he was quick. I swore he was deformed with at least ten fists and all of them coming at my belly and chin at the same time.

That's when I got my first taste of Tennessee sour mash whiskey. When I woke up, my lips and tongue were set on fire. "Wake up, kid!" he yelled, pouring more booze into my mouth.

When my eyes quit being all blurred up, I spewed and sputtered trying t'get my breath. "What is that stuff?" I yelled, struggling to get up.

He held up the jug for me t'see. "Jack Daniels, ain't none better."

Well, the taste of sour mash kept lingering on my tongue

until I just had t'have another swig. Jake was real free with his jug that day. In fact, he sat down on the floor beside me and we kilt it while he told me how he'd won his boots and gold-trimmed sombrero.

I took to ol' Jake like good times takes t'whiskey. And I reckon he took a shine t'me, too. We became gambling partners from that day on. He taught me how to turn any game of poker to my favor by more ways than a crow had for pilfering a corncrib. At first, we played together on his money at the same table so's he could show me all the tricks. He said I learned real fast and had the smarts to be a top player. It wasn't long till I was running my own table and pocketing more money every day than Pa got for burying one of Casper's rich folks.

And then there was the dancing with the perfumed gals from upstairs over the saloon. The first time I hugged one of them *soiled doves* was the day Jake dropped a dollar chip into Smokey Bill's hat. Smokey Bill, he was the guitar player, flashed a couple o' his gold teeth at Jake and said, "Hot?"

"Make it hotter than a jalapeno pepper. It's time the kid learned to jingle them spurs o' his."

Soon as Smokey Bill cut loose on his guitar, Jake opened the stairway door and yelled, "Maggie, it's dancing time. Bring Rosa for the kid."

Maggie and Rosa were the two best-looking gals that entertained the boys upstairs. Maggie was Jake's pick of the lot for dancing and upstairs frolicking, too. Every night after Jake had pocketed his winnings, they'd dance until Smokey Bill couldn't play any more. Then him and Maggie went upstairs for the rest of the night.

"I don't know how t'dance," I said, pocketing my winning's.

He shoved all the tables aside. "Just watch me. Ain't anything to it."

Before I could object, Maggie and Rosa came bounding down the stairs. Jake tossed his sombrero onto the barroom floor, grabbed Maggie's hand, and they began to dance around and around his sombrero. While he stamped his boots, she spun away until her skirt flew up exposing most all of her unmentionables. That's when I began to get calico fever.

I took t'dancing the flamingo just like I'd taken to poker. At first, Rosa got her toes busted a few times before I learned to do the proper steps. But it wasn't long before my spurs were jingling just like Jake's, and Rosa was making her skirt fly higher'n Maggie's. The following weeks I spent with Jake at the saloon playing poker, drinking sour mash, and dancing with Rosa turned me into an abomination to my ma. At least that's what she said I'd become.

I was hard headed as a prospector's burro. All of Ma's pleading and weeping didn't sway me from my sinful ways. Pa tried t'rein me in, but I stuck out my chest, chawed on my cud, and near spat in his eye when I told him where he could go. "Get out," he yelled. "And don't come back."

It all sadly came to an end one Saturday night not long after that. While Jake and I were having our dance with Maggie and Rosa, we didn't pay any attention to the shadowy figure that snuck in the back door. We'd been dancing so long that we were all blowing real hard and the sweat was stinging my eyes. The first thing I knew anything was wrong was when I heard Maggie scream. That's when Pa's big hogleg he kept in a dresser drawer went off right next to my ear. Jake didn't have time to do anything before his spurs stopped jingling for good.

The jury only considered Ma's fate for about ten minutes. I watched Marshal Tigman knuckle his mustache a couple of times while he was whispering to Pa before the jury pronounced their verdict. Pa had seemed to be upbeat during the trial after Tigman testified he'd received a wanted flyer on Jake Tillie. He'd got it the day after Pa buried Jake out on Boot Hill. Ma didn't know it, but she was due the one-hundred-dollar reward promised by the family of Juan Martinez for the capture, dead or alive, of Jake Tillie.

When the jury returned, Pa gripped my arm so tight I wanted to yell. The judge nodded at the jury, and then they sat down. "Who's the foreman?" he asked, peering over his spectacles.

Smokey Bill stood up to face the judge. "I am, your honor."

"Has the jury reached a verdict?"

"We have, your honor."

The judge looked squarely at Ma. "Mrs. Geiger, please stand up and face the jury."

Lawyer Slater, who argued that Ma had been temporarily insane when she kilt Jake, stood up as Pa helped Ma to stand. I'll never forget how she looked standing there all teary eyed, holding onto Pa and Slater's arms. Her mood was as black as her hair that didn't contain a single strand of gray in spite of all the misery I'd dealt her. She was a handsome woman, so said the *Casper Weekly Mail* reporter the day she was charged with the murder of Jake Tillie.

"And what is your verdict?" the judge said.

Smokey Bill looked right at me, instead of at Ma when he answered. "We find the defendant, Mrs. Sarah Geiger, **guilty** of voluntary manslaughter in the demise of Jake Tillie," he said, and then pointed his finger right at me. "That's because that brat o' hers drove her t'do it."

Ma near collapsed. Pa eased her down into a chair, and the judge stared right at me. He took off his spectacles and wagged his head before he spoke. "Mrs. Geiger," he said, sounding real sorry for what he had to do. "A jury of your peers has found you guilty of voluntary manslaughter. It is the duty of this court to sentence you to five years in the state penitentiary. However, the court sees fit to be merciful. Your sentence is reduced to six-months probation and a fine of two-hundred dollars."

Ma busted out in tears and Pa gave out a loud whoopee, which the judge ignored as he turned his eyes toward me. "Young man," he said, reaching for his big oak gavel. "Your ma's fine is your responsibility. I'll be seeing you in my chambers."

Doctor Magic's Medicine Wagon

I ain't likely to forget the day that Doc Ruby showed up in Casper driving one of them newfangled hossless carriages built by the Duryea brothers. It happened the day that I was down at old Zeke Tutwilder's livery looking at an appaloosa he had for sale. Y'see, I'd been taking a powerful lot of ribbing from all the boys around Casper about my brass spurs. That's because I didn't have a hoss to ride, which they said made my spurs about as useful as spectacles on a blind pig. I was sick o' their taunting, so I decided to do a little haggling with Zeke for one of his highbred appaloosas.

I was acting like I knew how to judge a hoss by looking at its teeth when the clanking sound of Doc's motorized buggy wheeled down the main drag. He was pulling a trailer built on buggy wheels and painted up like a circus wagon. The thing was all yellow with big red lettering clean across its side, which said, "Doctor Magic's Medicine Wagon."

Well now, my hoss inspection came to a halt and I sent my spurs t'jingling along with everybody else behind that smoking contraption. Every cowboy that was wetting his snout in White's Saloon came a running as Doc drove by. He doffed his Stetson at the *soiled doves* leaning out of their upstairs windows, and waved at the gathering crowd as he parked in front of Pa's store.

"Y'going t'tie that clattertrap to the hitching post, Doc," a cowboy wag astride a bay gelding yelled as Doc unfolded himself out of his motor buggy. "No need," Doc said, "if you boys will keep a keen eye on her and yell the moment she bellows."

"What's she sound like?" the wag replied. "When she bellers, that is."

Doc squeezed the rubber bulb on his horn a couple of

times, which sent that wag's hoss a bucking like a rodeo bronco. He kept bucking and snorting until a goodly portion of blue sky separated him from that cowboy's bounding posterior. That's when an ornery streak in Doc surfaced. He just kept squeezing his horn and laughing until the cowboy and his hoss went different ways. The gelding skedaddled and the wag got a mouthful of Casper dirt.

It had been eight years since I last saw Doc, but I'd of known him anywhere. His hair, mustache and beard had grayed some, but he looked the same with the exception of a black leather patch he was wearing over his right eye. As he stepped up on the boardwalk, that left eye of his settled on my countenance. "Well, I'll be, don't I know you?"

"Yes, sir," I said, throwing back my shoulders. "I'm Thomas Geiger."

Doc eyed my six-foot-two frame that some said was lanky as a newborn colt. "Ah, yes, little Tommy." Then he pushed up the brim of his hat and scratched his noggin. "Y'sure have grown up from the little runt I treated for the measles."

I stuck out my skinny chest a bit more. "Yes, sir, I'm eighteen now."

He eyed my bandied legs like he was fixing to toss out a diagnosis. "Rickets!" he said, wagging his noggin. "Looks like your ma didn't give you cod-liver oil like I told her to."

Well, I didn't want t'tell Doc what she said when he and Aunt Jane skedaddled out of Lander. It was something like no real Doctor would do a thing like that, so she threw out all the medicine bottles with his name on 'em. I didn't mind much, because that included a bottle of cod-liver oil that smelled like a rotten fish.

"Is your ma still the gossiping queen of Wyoming?" he ast, searching me with his bloodshot left eye. Well, he didn't expect an answer I reckon, because he kept on a talking. "Her and that friend of hers... uh, what was her name?"

"Miss Lightfoot."

"Yeah, Elberta 'Bigmouth' Lightfoot—that old biddy and your ma had idle minds and flapping tongues to boot."

There's no denying what Doc said, because it was a fact.

Doc and I got reacquainted right there on the boardwalk in front of Pa's store and funeral parlor. When I ast him about his right eye being covered with a patch, he said that his eye got put out the day Aunt Jane and he parted company. It seems that she had opened a hog ranch; that's what us cowboys called a bawdyhouse, y'know. Her place was down where the old stage road between Rawlins and Lander crossed the Sweetwater River. Her clientele were most of the cowboys working the ranches scattered for a lot'a miles up and down the Sweetwater. They nearly always paid her and her gals for their services with branded yearlings and a few mavericks that hadn't got branded yet.

Well, that brings me to what happened to Doc's right eye. One day, several of the ranchers whose yearlings were grazing in Aunt Jane's pasture came calling. She and Doc had learned how to change brands with a running iron from one of the cowboys working for the Bar-Six ranch. Later on, they found out that changing brands was not only a ticklish procedure, but also one that could result in a busted neck at the end of a lariat slung over a tree limb. Well, those ranchers walked their hosses across Aunt Jane's pasture counting boogered brands. It seems that by the time they got done, they were madder than a pack of hounds that had been outsmarted by a conniving old fox.

Doc had built a store 'bout a half mile from Aunt Jane's hog ranch where he peddled laudanum, whiskey, beer, and a few shelves filled with canned goods. Oh, of course, he did some doctoring, too. According to him, it didn't make any difference whether the patient was a human or some other species. He treated cowboys with the social diseases, hosses with the glanders, and helped with birthing balky younguns of women and mares alike. Well, the only thing that salvaged his hide that day was that he'd saved Hoss George from the ravages of syphilis ol' Hoss had caught down in Denver.

There were five o' them ranchers, including Hoss George, that called on Doc after they tied up Aunt Jane and tossed her screaming onto a buckboard. When they drove into Doc's yard, he heard Aunt Jane squealing like a pig with its snout caught in a slop bucket. When Doc ran out on the porch, men bent on quick justice aimed five Winchesters at him. "Just slip that hogleg out and drop it," Hoss George yelled. "Then y'can join your partner on the buckboard."

Doc didn't have any choice in the matter, so he did like he was told. Aunt Jane kept yelling at Doc t'get them out of their mess while the vigilante party was headed toward a grove of box elder trees. "What was I t'do?" Doc said to me. "We was hogtied and headed for a hanging."

Then I ast 'im, "What happened next?"

He said that when they reached the grove of trees, Hoss picked out the best one for the job at hand. After slinging two lariats over a low limb, they got Doc and Aunt Jane off the buckboard and onto a couple of hosses. Aunt Jane kept yelling all sorts of obscenities at Hoss George while he slipped the nooses around her and Doc's necks. "I sure hate t'hang ya, Doc," George said, "but changing brands like you two did don't get passed over."

"With those parting words, one of the ranchers fired his Winchester into the air and yelled, "Hah! Git!"

Well, Doc said that he didn't come around for quite a spell, because he'd cracked his noggin on the frozen ground. Apparently, Hoss George had cut Doc's lariat just as the Winchester bellered. Aunt Jane didn't get off that easy. Her corpse twisting in the wind was what Doc first saw when he waked up.

Hoss didn't cut the rope soon enough to keep it from snapping across Doc's face, which resulted in a deep rope burn that blinded his right eye. The incident convinced Doc that he had to change his ways, so he decided to start his own medicine show.

Just as he started to tell me about his show, Ma came walking down the boardwalk. At first, Doc didn't recognize her, 'cause she was wearing a big plumed hat that nearly hid her face. When she got close enough for Doc to see who she was, he let out with a big breathy swearword. "Damnation," he said, blowing his breath right into my face. Well, I couldn't believe my nose. Doc's breath was as sweet as a newborn baby's. I started t'ast him how he got rid of his stink, but Ma had his undivided attention.

Ma was real good at insulting folks when she took a mind to. She tilted her head to one side and said, "Get away from that man, Tommy. He's a quack and a scoundrel."

I glanced at Doc, but he acted like he hadn't heard what she said. "Good morning Mrs. Geiger," he said, doffing his Stetson.

Ma stopped, stared at Doc and tossed back her head like she did when a scolding was about to scoot off her tongue. "Doctor Ruby! Either you get out of Casper or I'll tell Marshal Tigman who you are."

Ma's threat didn't faze Doc. He pulled out two tickets to his show and handed them to her, which she refused to accept. "Now, Mrs. Geiger," Doc crooned, trying t'sweet talk her. "I'm going to tell all you good folks in Casper about my new miracle cure at the show today."

"Miracle cure" got Ma's attention right away. She glanced at my bandied legs, which some said was bowed wide enough for a fat hog to scoot between. "Miracle, did you say, Doctor Ruby?"

That's when Doc began to grin. "Why, yes indeed," he said, plopping his big hand on my shoulder. "My new elixir will prolong life, clear blemished skin, cure ague, stop bilious attacks, sweeten halitosis, straighten bowed legs, and heal most all of the infirmities suffered by womankind."

"Do tell!" Ma said, batting her eyes.

"Yes ma'am," Doc said, holding out his tickets again.

Ma hesitated, but then she took the tickets. "Thank you, Doctor Ruby, I'll speak with Mister Geiger about your miracle cure."

"The show begins at two o'clock," Doc called as Ma walked into the store.

* * *

Doc's show was a sight to behold. He was dressed up in a black cape lined with red satin just like a magician I'd seen down at Denver. He started by giving his speech about how he discovered the essence of the balm of Gilead during a trip to the

Valley of Kings in Egypt. He claimed to have happened onto the secret while studying hieroglyphics inscribed on the tomb of a pharaoh. The formula, which was called the elixir of eternal youth, was given credit for the pharaoh's life span of one hundred and fifteen years.

All the time Doc was talking up his elixir, he was doing magic tricks with all sorts of props. Birds, rabbits, flowers, and bottles of elixir popped out of his Stetson. And then they would disappear just a quickly. His act was followed by card tricks that really caught my eye. I decided right there to ast him to teach me the ones I could use playing poker.

Well now, Doc's method of hawking his magic elixir snared the crowd like fish gulping hooked bait. His finale was a real ripsnorter that had everyone fighting to get their hands on a bottle of his eternal youth. Doc blew a whistle and waved at the painted wagon. The entire side opened up and there stood the purtiest gal my eyes had ever lain on. She was tall as me and had all her female parts in the right places. Her hair was black as one of Pa's ebony caskets, and she was wearing belly-dancing clothes that exposed a goodly portion of skin. To top it all off she had a big red ruby in her bellybutton that flashed as she began to dance. Then as she gyrated her hips, Doc laid it on the folks. Her name was Fatima, and she was from the land of the Nile where she had been dancing for fifty-two years. "That's right folks," Doc bellered. "Fatima is seventy years old, but she doesn't look more than twenty-five does she? Just look how nimble and quick she is doing her steps. That's because she's on her third bottle of my magic elixir."

Well, every one of those folks surged toward Doc just itching t'trade a silver dollar for a bottle of eternal youth. Even Ma bought three bottles. Reckon she figured if three did that for Fatima, she'd be looking eighteen again in a couple of weeks. I even bought one after Doc said it had cured his halitosis. But, I found out later that wasn't the truth. He had simply stopped eating Limburger cheese and chasing it with medicinal brandy.

Now this brings me to how I tried to get together with Doc in show business. I sort of thought Doc's entire pitch was a sham at the start, but his show changed my mind. That's how convincing he was. I could see he was on a course that was going t'make him a rich man. Old greed began to seduce me so much after his show that I decided to ast Doc whether he needed a helper. We talked well into the night at White's Saloon about my joining his show.

The whiskey and Doc's pride about conning folks got him bragging how he came up with his scheme to separate folks from their dollars. His so-called magic elixir was nothing more than olive oil with licorice and a tad of oil of wintergreen added. As it turned out, the whole idea started with Fatima's belly dancing. Oh, her name really wasn't Fatima, and the closest she'd ever been to Egypt and the Nile was Cheyenne, Wyoming. Her real name was Jennie and she was one of the gals that worked at the Cheyenne Club. That's where all the Cheyenne cattle barons and their guests partied. Doc met her there one night when he was the guest of an old friend, Henry MacSpaddin. "Jennie's belly dancing was a sight that made me forget all about Aunt Jane," Doc said, while sipping whisky. "I was struck with a compelling desire to get her out of the Cheyenne Club and into my own service."

I knew right away what Doc meant. That's what Ma called cohabitation. He noticed that I was having a hard time keeping my eyes off of Fatima. He leaned over and whispered into my ear. "Y'can look, Tommy, but y'can't touch."

"Yes sir," I said, glancing down at my whiskey glass.

Doc laughed at my embarrassment and slapped me on the back. "Don't fret none, we'll find you a dancing gal, too."

I had no doubt about his meaning; he was going to take me into his show business. "Whoopie," I said, nearly turning over my whiskey glass while reaching t'shake his hand. "I'll work hard at doing whatever y'want."

As we sat there celebrating, I immediately thought of Rosa. I could just imagine how she'd look dressed up like Fatima and with a ruby stuck in her bellybutton. I began to dream about making all that money and getting to cohabit some myself.

Ma was thrown into one of her twits when I told her what I was going t'do. I reckon Pa was tired of my wayward ways, so he gave me a lecture about staying out of trouble. But, when he'd finished telling me that I was associating with the devil and would come to a bad end, he accepted my decision.

The following morning at first light, I went down to White's Saloon to ast Rosa to go with me. At first, she was real reluctant, but then when I promised her how much money we were going to make, she packed her stuff.

Rosa and I walked down to Zeke Tutwilder's livery; that's where Doc and Jennie were spending the night in Doc's trailer. When we reached Tutwilder's corral, Doc's hossless buggy and trailer weren't anywhere t'be seen. I about tore down Zeke's door with my fist, trying to wake him up. Zeke finally opened the door.

"Where's Doc Ruby?"

Ol' Zeke stood there in his nightshirt all disheveled and red-eyed a staring at me. "He ain't here."

"I can see that," I yelled in his face. "Where is he?"

"Gone."

"Gone where?"

"He didn't say."

The most humiliating day of my life had dawned. It wasn't Rosa's laughing that got to me the most, it was having to tell Ma that she was never going to look eighteen again.

A Tough Bounty Hunter

Pa had long before reconciled himself to my rebellious ways, but Ma was different. Like most mothers, she had decided early on as to what I was going to be after I'd grown to manhood. I reckon she'd made up her mind that I wasn't going to follow in Pa's footsteps and become a mortician. Well, she needn't have bothered because I'd decided that myself. I suppose it was the smell of formaldehyde that turned me against the whole thing. Pa seemed to have figured out how to cope by smoking cheroots while he was embalming folks. He learned that trick from ol' Ezra Tykes who was a furniture and casket salesman out o' Laramie. It was him that sold Pa on embalming his clients with formaldehyde. I guess it was to please the sophisticated folks that were moving into Casper after the Fremont and Elkhorn Railroad came to town. Ol' Ezra pointed out to Pa that there weren't any flowers growing in Wyoming during the winter. Consequently, there wasn't any fragrant blooms to sweeten the air during a wintertime funeral; a situation that irked the hanky-patting ladies living on the high ground in Casper's New Town. A goodly gush of formaldehyde into the veins of the deceased made for a better atmosphere in the church while the parson waxed eloquent about the departed. I think Ezra gave Pa good advice; however, even when I smoked one of Pa's cheroots I couldn't abide the smarting eyes and weeping nose that afflicted any poor soul unlucky enough to be a modern mortician.

Ma's idea didn't set with me concerning the vocation she wanted me to follow. Becoming a judge was her idea of a profession that would make me into the kind of son she could brag about at her guild meetings. Well, just sitting in a courtroom until you got rump-sprung listening to them that called themselves lawyers, and then passing out sentences that kept y'looking over your shoulder wasn't for me. And before getting t'be a judge, you had to read law with a genuine lawyer until the Supreme Court decided you could call yourself a bonafide barrister. That held no interest for me. I yearned to be a lawman, not like Marshal Tigman who sat in his office all day eating nuts and sorting wanted posters. I wanted to have a fast gun hand like Wyatt Earp or Wild Bill Hickok. I figured they were genuine officers of the law that had no fear of being beat by an outlaw's draw.

But I had no other place to start my career, so I decided on asking Tigman to hire me. He was sitting behind that big oak desk of his when I walked into his office. He had aged a mite since we moved to Casper back in 1890. The afternoon sun shining through the window highlighted his Earp-like mustache and disheveled shock of hair, both white as the rump of an antelope. His eyes, dimmed by age, peered at me over pinch-nosed spectacles. I doffed my Stetson, fingered the brim, and glanced about the room to avoid his penetrating stare. I managed to clear my throat a couple of times before he spoke.

"Well, son, speak up!"

"Yes, sir, I ah…."

He stared at me and said nothing while he knuckled his mustache, smiled, and leaned back in his chair.

"I want t'be a lawman," I said, my voice squeaking like Ma's when she got into a twit over something me or Pa had done.

"That's commendable," he said, removing his spectacles. "You wanting t'work for me—is that why you're here?"

"Yes, sir."

"You good with a mop and broom?"

"Huh?" I blurted, a'taken back by what that had to do with being a lawman.

He tongued his chaw of tobacco and spat into an old spittoon setting next t'his chair. "I got a deputy, but I could use a jailer," he said, wiping brown spittle from his mustache. "Part of your job would be to clean up the office and jail."

I strained to be a bit taller and thrust out my skinny chest. "Is that all?"

Tigman stood up and reached for a holstered Colt .45 and cartridge belt hanging behind his desk. He tossed it to me and told me to strap it on. I fumbled trying to cinch the belt around my waist. There just weren't enough holes to accommodate my lanky girth. I wanted to get it just right because I thought he was hiring me on the spot. The belt was so loose that the holster slid low on my hip, which I figured was the way a lawman should wear one anyhow.

"Now," he said, "that gun ain't loaded, so don't think you're going t'shoot me."

"Huh?" I said, questioning what Tigman had in mind.

"Take your time," he drawled, "whenever you're ready, see if you can outdraw me. I won't move until you start for leather."

"How about yours?" I said, barely above a whisper. "Is it loaded?"

"Yeah, but I won't pull the trigger. Anytime you're ready, son."

I knew this was my big chance to show off the results of my practicing with Pa's Colt. I was convinced that I could out draw the decrepit old man I was facing. My hand nearly got to the walnut grips of the .45 when Tigman slapped leather and I stood there staring down the muzzle of his gun.

"I'm a lot slower now than when I was your age," he said and jammed his Colt back into its holster. "You want the jailer's job or not?"

Well, I reckon my pride took a second look at my predicament. It appeared like Tommy Geiger, that's me y'know, was about two notches above a lizards belly. Being the town jailer in Casper, Wyoming was a fair distance from wearing a lawman's badge and commanding the respect of upright citizens and outlaws alike.

While I stood there pondering my decision, Tigman went back to sorting his wanted posters. He had two stacks on his desk. One was WANTED DEAD OR ALIVE, while the other was just WANTED. When I looked right close at the dead or alive stack, a familiar face peered back at me from the one on top. At first, I couldn't believe what I was seeing. But there wasn't any mistake about the hombre whose right eye was covered with a black leather patch. It was Doc Ruby. "What's Doc wanted for?" I asked, reaching for the poster.

He grabbed my wrist. "Murder!"

"Murder? Who'd he do in?"

"His dancer. That poster came in this morning from the marshal up at Deadwood.

"Fatima? Doc kilt Fatima?"

"Reckon so—he's a hard case if I ever met one."

Old devil greed sort of stirred my soul right then; besides, Doc had run out on me after he agreed to make me a partner in his medicine show. "Can I take a look at the small print on that poster?"

"Reckon y'can, since you asked proper."

Written below Doc's picture were just two short sentences. *One hundred dollars reward for the capture of Doc Ruby, dead or alive, for the murder of his dancing girl, Fatima. The reward can be collected from Marshal Hank Carter, Deadwood, South Dakota.*

My pondering reminded me that capturing ol' Doc would be getting me more than a hundred bucks. It would open the door to my becoming a badge-wearing, outlaw-catching lawman—maybe even United States Marshal Tom Geiger. Now that had a right smart ring to it. From that moment on I decided to drop the Tommy moniker that Ma and Pa had tagged on me. I would be Tom. Folks would come to respect Tom Geiger. About that time, Tigman interrupted my dreaming. "Well, are ya or ain't y'wanting the jailer's job?"

I handed the poster back to him. "Reckon I ain't.".

He glanced at it and then at me. He read my thoughts like a swami. "Now, Tommy, better leave the bounty hunting t'the fast guns. Y'ain't up to it. Take the jailer's job."

After talking him out of Doc's wanted poster, I left Tigman's office in high spirits. His snide quip didn't faze me. I was going t'buy one of Zeke Tutwilder's appaloosas, strap on Pa's holster and hogleg, and ride for fame and fortune at first light the next morning.

Pa was glad to see me ride out, but Ma flew into one of

her twits. "Do something, Mister Geiger," she screeched as I stepped into my stirrup. "I just know Tommy won't be coming back."

Her shrill voice sent my appaloosa into a bucking fit. "Whoa, you knothead," I yelped, yanking back the reins, but he was intent upon planting my butt in the dust of Casper's main drag. I grabbed the saddle horn, clamped my spindly legs around his ribs, and raked him a couple of times with my silver-rowel spurs. I figured that would show him who was boss. He was dumber or maybe smarter than I thought because he just bucked harder until I reckon he decided it wasn't working. That's when he headed north hell bent for leather. He galloped full out down the road toward the Platte River Bridge. By the time he ran out of piss and vinegar, we had crossed the bridge and left Ma and Pa and the white picket fence around our yard far behind.

* * *

About a week later, I reined ol' Spider, that's what Tutwilder said my appaloosa's name was, up to the hitching rail in front of Marshal Carter's office in Deadwood. I stepped out of my stirrup and flipped ol' Spider's reins around the hitching rail. I made certain that Pa's Colt .45 and holster was riding low on my hip. I wanted to look the part of a tough and experienced bounty hunter. I'd even let my scraggly crop of whiskers go unshaved while I was traveling, trying t'look a mite older than my 19 years. I needn't have done it because Marshal Carter recognized my tender years right away. "Howdy," I drawled, stepping through the doorway. "My name is Tom Geiger."

"What can I do for you, sonny," he said without looking up from a ledger he was writing in.

"Y'still wanting this feller?" I said, tossing Doc's wanted poster on his desk.

He stopped writing and glanced at Doc's picture. He leaned back in his swivel chair and looked at me with a stare that sent a chill slithering up my spine. He didn't say a word, just sat there with those steely eyes sizing up my slab-sided physique. I could tell from the grin that lifted his neatly trimmed mustache that he wasn't impressed by what he saw. Finally, he slid open a desk drawer, pulled out a ring of keys, and stood up, all seven feet of him. He wasn't only taller than Doc Ruby, but he was also a hulking specimen of humanity.

"Come with me, sonny," he said, motioning toward a hallway with four barred cells at the end.

I know he figured that I thought he was going t'lock me up when I wagged my head and refused t'budge. "Come on, sonny," he said, reassuring me with a pat on the shoulder. "I just want t'show you something."

I wasn't sure of his good intentions, but I didn't have any other option except to high tail it out of Deadwood. And that would have been a stupid decision since he held the reward money for whoever apprehended Doc. So, I followed him down the hall toward whatever awaited my wary soul.

Marshal Carter unlocked the door at the end of the hall and motioned for me to follow him. I could see that it wasn't a jail cell, just a dark room without any windows. He struck a match and lit a lantern hanging on a wall peg. When that yellow flame lit up the room, I came real close to getting out o' town. There was a new pine coffin sitting on two sawhorses in the middle of the room. The marshal pried off the lid with a crowbar, leaned it against the wall, and motioned for me to step closer. I relaxed about then 'cause I'd seen a lot of dead folks in my pa's funeral parlor. "Doc's dead?" I asked, staring at the marshal.

"Might be," he said, nudging me to take a look. "Do you know Doc Ruby?"

I leaned over t'get a good look. "Yes, sir,"

Marshal Carter held the lantern over the coffin so I could better see the deceased. He was tall, and had on a long, black frock coat like Doc always wore. Then I looked at his face. My legs went weak when I saw a big black patch covering his left eye. I could see my reward money and future as a lawman flying away on the wings of fate. Then I remembered—Doc's right eye was the one that the vigilante's rope had blinded down on the Sweetwater when they tried to hang him and Aunt Jane. "That ain't Doc Ruby," I yelled, taking a real close gander at the departed's features.

"Y'certain that ain't Ruby?"

"Yes, sir, I'm sure."

Marshal Carter nailed the lid back on the coffin, and then we walked back to his office. I was back in business—so I thought.

"You're right certain he ain't Doc Ruby?"

"Yes, sir."

"I don't take kindly to liars—'specially lying bounty hunters," he said, tapping his finger against my chest.

"I ain't lying. Doc was blind in his right eye."

"That the only reason y'say that ain't Doc Ruby."

"No, sir. That feller has pock scars all over his face. Doc never had the pox."

The marshal nodded and sat down. He picked up Doc's wanted poster and gave the picture a good looking over.

"Well, I'll be damned, sonny," he drawled. "Reckon you're a better detective than I am. Y'caught the patch being over the wrong eye right off and you're right about Ruby's face."

My spirits soared from the marshal's brag on me. The visions of my being a U. S. marshal caused me to stand taller. "Well, sir, I'll be back to collect Doc's reward soon as I find him," I said and patted the Colt hanging low on my hip.

Carter leaned back in his chair and wagged his head. "I gave all but twenty-five dollars of the reward to Jake Turpin this morning after he rode in with that corpse slung across his pack mule. The twenty-five is for the pine box he's laid out in."

"Who's Jake Turpin?" I ast, not sure I really wanted to know.

"Jake's a bounty hunter—meaner than a rabid wolf."

Now I realized if I brought Doc in, most likely dead since he'd not come willing, there wasn't any reward money left. And Doc wasn't any slouch when it came to shooting his big nickel-plated Remington .44 with an extra long barrel. He'd kilt Aunt Jane's macaw, ol' Polly Boy, with a single shot from ten feet without even aiming at him. And I was a whale of a lot bigger than Polly Boy. While I was standing there pondering what to do, Marshal Carter stuck Doc's wanted poster in my face and gave me some advice. "If I was you, sonny, I'd hightail it out of Deadwood. Y'ain't no match for Jake Turpin."

I folded the poster, stuck it in my pocket, and offered my hand for a departing shake with Marshal Carter. His eyes bored into mine conveying a message that didn't need any words or explanation. He was plainly saying that he would need another twenty-five-dollar pine box for my carcass if I tangled with Jake Turpin over the reward money. My eyes in turn silently spoke my mind back to him. *I ain't riding back t'Casper without the reward money for capturing Doc Ruby. I just couldn't bear listening to the humiliating guffaws of Marshal Tigman.* So, I didn't have any other choice but to confront Jake Turpin. "Turpin's most likely over at the White Dove Saloon," Marshal Carter said as I turned to leave. "Y'd better hope he's too drunk t'slap leather."

I had passed the White Dove Saloon out on the edge of town as I rode into Deadwood. I took special notice of it 'cause it was right across the road from the Lutheran Church. I wondered if the hymn singing by the good church folks and the rowdy piano tunes coming from the saloon on Sunday morning would be upsetting for the patrons of both establishments. I guess I'd forgotten that it was Sunday morning as I reined ol' Spider down the main drag. But I got reminded right off when I heard the good saints raising their voices in song. It was a warm summer day and they had all the church's windows open so they could sweat out an hour of the parson waxing eloquent.

There were a goodly number of buggy rigs and saddled horses tied to the hitching rails in front of the church and the saloon. Then I noticed something amiss. There wasn't any sounds coming from the saloon, no thumping piano keys, no rowdy voices, nothing. I stepped out of my stirrup and sauntered up on the planked sidewalk and peered through one of the saloon's windows. There was nary a soul inside. Then I saw a poster on the front door. CLOSED UNTIL CHURCH IS OVER.

Reckon I was about as relieved as I was upset over the situation. I pulled out the pocket watch Ma and Pa had given me for Christmas, flipped open the cover and saw that it was fifteen minutes past eleven. The abiding question in my mind was just when the Lutheran folks would be heading home. We didn't have any Lutheran church in Casper, just Catholic, Episcopalian, and Methodist. The Catholics and Episcopalians got done by noon, but the Methodists sort of stayed on until either the spirit or hunger urged them t'shut down. Well, the sun was high and the day was getting right hot, too hot t'wait without any shade. That's when I decided to go t'church and wait for my showdown with Jake Turpin.

Nobody noticed as I slid my butt into the back pew, not even the corpulent lady I sat next to. The windows were wide open but there was a steady whirring of muscle-powered fans by most all of the ladies. The men just wiped the sweat from their faces with bandannas. No he-man would be caught dead waving a church fan.

The singing ended just as I sat down, and then the parson stood up and stepped behind a big oak pulpit. He did all of the proper procedures he was supposed to, I reckon. Ma and Pa were Methodists and I guess I was too, since I got baptized when I was only a few days old. I'm afraid I went astray when I was about 16 or 17. My cavorting around with Jake Tillie and the soiled doves caused my ma t'drag me to church every Sunday morning after she kilt ol' Jake with Pa's hogleg. That sort of turned me against socializing with all them pious folks, so I rebelled against Ma's mothering. I just refused t'go anymore after meeting up with Doc Ruby and his dancing girl, Fatima.

My mind sort of drifted out the window during the parson's sermon. That's what I always did when the chastising came spewing out of a preacher's mouth. I wasn't ready to mend my ways. No sir, I was going t'be my own man and become a genuine U. S. marshal. After that, I might start squirming in the pew again.

While the preacher was bestowing his departing blessings on all us folks, I got up and sent my spurs t'jingling out the door. I got about halfway down the front steps when I felt a firm grip on my right shoulder. Before I could turn around, another hand relieved my holster of Pa's Colt that had silenced ol' Jake Tillie's spurs. "Don't try nothing or I'll drop y'right here," a stranger said, shoving me toward the saloon.

"Who're you?" I yelled.

"Jake Turpin!"

I tried to face him, but Turpin kept shoving me towards the saloon. My bandy legs couldn't keep up with all that shoving which caused me to stumble and fall flat on my belly. Before I could get my breath, Turpin grabbed a fistful of my shirt and yanked me to my feet. He spun me around and got his mangy beard right into my face. His bloodshot eyes were about six inches from mine when he sent shivers down my spine with his menacing stare. "I hear tell you're a lying slab-sided snot?"

"Huh—Me?"

"Yeah, you! Carter says I faked killing Doc Ruby and I gotta give back the reward."

"He—He did?

"Yeah—He did, and he said you was the one claiming that corpse ain't Doc Ruby."

I tried t'back away from his foul whiskey breath, but he kept coming at me. That's when I planted my right knee into his crotch with all the power I could muster. If you've ever seen the eyes of a steer getting his butt branded, you'll know just how Turpin looked as he screamed, grabbing for his tortured parts. "You little bastard," he yelled as my left knee found a home in his groin. That's when I high tailed it to ol' Spider, untied his reins and straddled him in one leap.

Ol' Spider and me were headed full out toward Casper for several miles afore I reined him down to an easy canter. I nearly got a crick in my neck from looking over my shoulder t'see whether Jake Turpin was in sight. Well, he never caught up with me. I guess he didn't need to since I couldn't sign papers saying the man he kilt wasn't Doc Ruby.

Well, I reckon the better side of my being a bounty hunter looking for Doc Ruby was that he was dead and buried in a pine box on boot hill outside of Deadwood, South Dakota. Well, not really dead, but he was as far as the law was concerned. Marshal Carter wasn't about to admit his mistake and renege on the reward. Doc Ruby could now take on a new moniker and keep on hoodwinking folks.

The worst results of my being a bounty hunter was losing Pa's Colt and listening to Tigman say, "Told ya!

Sam Grace's Infernal Machine

My favorite place to read and learn about the world was in our "Relief Cottage" library. I never will forget all of those pictures in the Sears Roebuck catalog. One catalog usually lasted us about a year, so Ma always replenished the outhouse paper supply with last year's edition. We had other magazines and a copy of the *Casper Weekly Mail* as well—but my favorite was Harper's Monthly. That's where I saw my first picture of a motorcycle. It was a stylish, wire-wheeled machine called the Orient-Aster, built by the Metz Company in Waltham, Massachusetts. My consuming desire was to straddle one of those bellowing contraptions and show it off to everyone. But that wasn't to be, not just then.

Some folks said we had the most elaborate outhouse in Casper's New Town. The first thing Pa did after we moved from Lander to Casper was to build a four-holer about 25 yards back of our house. I never could figure out why he built one with four holes. In fact, I don't think half of them got used in one sitting. It never caught on for a crowd to gather inside at the same time. Ma insisted on having all the niceties of the day at her guests' disposal whenever they visited the "Relief Cottage". That was a name she coined for the *Casper Weekly Mail* reporter whenever he dropped by to write an article about our classy outhouse. Ordinarily, I don't reckon such would get much attention from any newspaper, but anything unusual that made its debut in Casper got touted on the front page. The reporter described all of Ma's accouterments gracing the "Relief Cottage", including a bucket of ashes, a varnished oak cabinet, soap dish, washbasin, dipper and pail of water, and a towel rack—all for the user's convenience. Magazines, newspapers, and a Sears Roebuck catalog were conveniently placed on shelves, all of them a source of entertainment as well as for other practical uses.

I was determined to preserve that picture of the Orient-Aster, so I tore it out of Harper's and tacked it to the wall where I could admire it on each visit. A lot of times, I tarried just so I could dream about riding one of those elegant machines. But all I could do was dream until I got older. In fact, it was a year after I returned to Casper from my encounter with Jake Turpin in Deadwood, South Dakota, when I finally realized my desire. That was the day Sam P. Grace roared into town astride a shining red Orient-Aster. He had a sign and a big Blackstone law book strapped behind the seat. What a sight that machine was. Old devil covet slipped into my gizzard that day.

Local gossipers claimed that the arrival of Samuel P. Grace increased the lawyer population of Casper to two and one-half. Of course, Ma was the principal source of this nasty chatter. She didn't hesitate to express her distaste for any professional who straddled such a foul contraption. Any dignified citizen, like a doctor, lawyer, preacher, or mortician, doing so should be tarred, feathered, and ridden out of town on a rail. Well, Sam didn't cotton to this backbiting rumor so he retaliated. He sued Ma along with the other ladies in her guild for malicious slander and defamation of character. Marshal Tigman broke the news to Ma when he dropped in on the ladies having tea at our house. "I'm real sorry, Mrs. Geiger," he said, handing the official document to her. "It seems you ladies have offended our new attorney."

Tigman's declaration disrupted our parlor like a swarm of bees attacking a honey-thieving bear. I think a couple of them who had a more delicate nature keeled over while searching for their smelling salts. That was the beginning of a very trying time in Casper.

* * *

My infatuation with motorcycles became a powerful influence on me after Sam Grace rode into town. It drove me to a number of extremes, the least of which was my determination to wangle a ride on his machine. Simply getting acquainted with the man that Ma and her gossip biddies had insulted was a difficult job requiring a bit of conniving on my part. After returning from my short career as a bounty hunter, Pa had insisted on my being a responsible, law abiding, and employed member of the Geiger household. Nobody else needed my limited talents, so he hired me to help him in the business of burying Casper's departed. I flat out refused to do any embalming because of the eye watering, nose burning, and coughing fits produced by formaldehyde fumes wafting up my nose. It became my job to provide most of the muscle for the Geiger Mortuary—digging graves, shining the funeral coach, tending the horses and hauling caskets from the Fremont, Elkhorn and Missouri Valley depot. That's when I had to develop some persuasive talents for the recruitment of gravediggers, which was no easy task, to dig holes deep enough for a casket in the rocky soil of Casper's graveyard. Digging graves most everyplace in Wyoming was a real sweat producer, even more so in the winter when the frozen ground was hard as a banker's heart.

I decided to drop in on Lawyer Grace about two months after Marshal Tigman served his lawsuit papers on Ma and the ladies guild. I figured if I could persuade men who were not always friends of the deceased to pick up a spade and pickaxe and head for boot hill, I ought to be able to finagle a ride on Sam's Orient-Aster. I paid my visit one evening while returning from the depot with a fancy cherry-wood casket loaded in the back of our funeral coach. The situation seemed right for my visit—the casket being intended for the remains of Mrs. Gladys Durwood-Baker, the widow of Shannon Baker who built Casper's first oil refinery. Granny Gladys, as most folks affectionately called her, had passed on only a week after Grace wrote out a last will and testament for her. Being the attorney for her estate, Sam requested a cherry-wood casket for Granny. After several telegrams sent by Pa to Denver and Cheyenne, he located one at the Denver Casket Company. They happily shipped it to us the next day for an extra fifty bucks. I figured Sam would like to check it out.

While he inspected the casket, I caressed Sam's motorcycle. Just thinking about that experience still sends messages of ecstasy plumb through me. Sam's Orient-Aster had the most tantalizing aromas. I hadn't known the subtle scents of oil and gasoline since Doc Ruby drove into Casper with his brand new Duryea brother's horseless carriage. It was like a waft of perfume I sniffed while climbing the stairs for my first visit with Rosa at White's Saloon. I gently stroked the handlebars, gas tank, spring-supported saddle and tires. Each touch stirred my determination more and more to throw a leg across her, grip those handlebars and roar off down the street in a cloud of dust. I was lost in ecstasy—longer than Sam considered proper, I reckon. He returned me from the land of rapture when I heard him say, "You can look, Tommy, but y'can't touch."

That brought back a troubling memory of the time Doc Ruby said the same thing while I was ogling his dancing girl, Fatima. "Yes, sir," I said, stepping away from his pride and joy. "That's the purtiest thing I've ever seen."

"She is a beauty," he said, pulled a silk handkerchief out of his pocket and proceeded to remove my finger smudges from the handlebars. "That's why I named her, Heavenly Machine."

"Yeah, she sure is—that's for certain. Can she go fast as a hoss?" I asked, gesturing speed by a swishing motion of my hand.

"Don't rightly know. I've never raced her, but she stirs up quite a blast of wind in my face."

"Golly," I said, eyeballing Heavenly Machine again. "I'd sure like t'ride her, just once."

"Yeah, I know the feeling, but nobody except me, Sam P. Grace, will ever straddle Heavenly Machine."

"Yes, sir," I said, retreating to the driver's seat of our funeral coach.

When I untied the reins and kicked off the brake lever, Grace climbed up and sat down beside me. "I tell y'what," he said, slapping my knee. "How fast is your appaloosa?"

"Spider can beat any hoss in Casper," I bragged.

"Want t'see whether he can beat Heavenly Machine?"

Now, that proposition grabbed my attention like the "dead man's hand", y'know the two pairs of aces and eights held by Wild Bill Hickok when he got kilt in Deadwood. "Reckon, I might," I said, pondering the possibilities.

"Okay! How about next Sunday afternoon?"

"Fine, where 'bouts?"

"We can start a mile east of town and have the finish line at the depot."

"A mile is a long way for a hoss t'run full out."

"Y'scared of getting beat by a one-cylindered motorcycle?"

He got me with that snide quip. I was real proud of ol' Spider. That hoss had a lot o' heart and could run like a tornado. "Ain't scared of any hoss or machine," I said, extending my hand to seal the deal.

"Now that we've agreed to race, we need to sweeten the pot."

"Pot? Y'mean we'll be racing for money?"

"Sure."

My composure got a real jolt by that proposition. It would be a month before Pa would compensate me for my services, and that would be a paltry sum after deducting room and board. "Sorry, ain't got no money t'bet."

"Well," he said, slipping his hand out of my weakening grip. "A race without a wager won't mean much. How about betting something of value?"

"Such as?"

"Your horse against my motorcycle—you win, you get Heavenly Machine."

"And if you win, you get ol' Spider?"

"How about it?"

While I scratched my noggin and pondered that proposition, Grace kept grinning. A growing dislike for that scheming lawyer was rising up in my gizzard. His love for Heavenly Machine was certain. He wasn't going to take a chance on losing her, so just what did he have up his sleeve? Y'know how lawyers use words to give y'something in one breath and then take it away with the next one, or confuse you so much that up and down gets swapped in your mind. I decided right then that I was going to do a little lawyering of my own. If I decided to wager ol' Spider against Grace's motorcycle, it was going to be spelled out in a signed agreement. There weren't going to be any whereas this and whereas that statements which require appeals all the way to the Supreme Court. No, sir, that wasn't going to happen.

"Well, Tommy," he finally said, trying to extract me from my deliberations. "What do you say? Is it a bet?"

I looked him square in the eye with the old Geiger gaze, the one Pa always used when he was collecting for a casket before loading the deceased into our funeral coach. He always said that he had t'get paid while tears were still on the cheeks of the bereaved, because it was too late when they reached the chin. "Only on my terms," I said, wagging my finger in his face. "You sign a bill of sale for Heavenly Machine to me and I'll sign one for ol' Spider to you. Then we'll have Marshal Tigman hold them until we finish the race. The winner gets the loser's bill of sale."

"Then the marshal burns the winner's bill of sale?"

"You got it."

"Done," Grace said, slapping my shoulder. "I'll draw up the bills of sale right now."

He jumped on that proposition too quick for my comfort. Just what was he up to? I felt like an old grizzly that had stepped into a trap when he started climbing a tree to raid a beehive. Well, it was no never mind, I'd made the terms and Grace agreed to them. So, I pondered my next move as I stared at a swarm of gnats orbiting one of Pa's horses. I had a sinking feeling right then, realizing my brain was no match for the conniving shyster sitting next t'me. "Okay," I squeaked, barely above a whisper.

Marshal Tigman agreed to hold the wagers provided we allowed him to set up all the details for the race. That suited me just fine, because I figured he would keep everything on the up and up. I could tell from a frown and puckered lips that the owner of Heavenly Machine wasn't too happy with that proposition, but we shook on it anyhow.

Tigman scheduled the race for the following Sunday afternoon at two o'clock. I had six days to get ol' Spider in shape for a gut-wrenching contest against a one-cylindered motorcycle. Also, Grace spent those days tinkering with Heavenly Machine. He devoted more time to that project than lawyering, which Ma said was a blessing in disguise for the good citizens of Casper. On the other hand, she got her nose in a tilt over my reckless behavior. Grace's motorcycle got a new name when I told her about the race. "What!" she screeched, "You agreed to risk losing your horse in a race against that shyster's Infernal Machine?"

Pa was just as appalled as Ma at my irresponsible actions. "You don't know how fast that infernal machine can go—yet you wagered Spider in a winner-take-all race. That's the dumbest decision any Geiger has ever made."

That putdown remark really smarted. I wanted t'beller like a yearling getting his rump labeled with sizzling-hot wrought iron, but I stuck out my skinny chest instead and vented my anger. "I'll show you. Ol' Spider will have Grace gulping his dust. Then you both can eat your words," I shrieked and bolted out the door.

I walked down to the pole shed where I sat down on a bale of hay t'ponder my woes. I soon realized that my rage came from Pa and Ma saying what was a fact. I had been suckered into a venture that would put me afoot after Sunday. While I was splashing around in a tub of self-pity like taking a bath on Saturday night, I reckon Pa decided he had to help me or Ma would turn our house into a quiet tomb. As tensions in our home rose, Ma would always turn on the silent treatment that was punctuated by sniffs, apron wringing, and mournful sighs. I suppose he decided I might have a chance if he helped get ol' Spider ready for the test. Whatever happened in the house while I was wallowing in depression caused him to walk down to the pole shed. "Go catch Spider," he said, patting me on the shoulder. "Let's get him ready for Sunday."

That week was the best time Pa and I ever had together. We both devoted every waking hour to toning up my appaloosa. Fortunately for me, none of the good or bad citizens of Casper required the services of the Geiger Mortuary before my encounter with Grace on Sunday. However, Ma stayed in a twit over the entire scenario. I was an irresponsible brat who refused to grow up and Pa was a sorry so and so for aiding and abetting my sinful ways. Both of us had to ignore her scornful glances and clucking tongue.

All the time Pa and I were training ol' Spider in the tactics of running a mile, my unworthy opponent was racing up and down all of the streets in Casper. Infernal Machine would come roaring through town, spewing acrid smoke and Casper dust behind its goggled rider. Oh, how I grew to hate him for his flaunting behavior. All of this activity was beginning to taunt Ma, causing her to threaten Pa and me. If ol' Spider lost on Sunday, she was leaving for Denver on the next train. She refused to answer when Pa asked her what on earth she would do in Denver. Even when Pa pointed out that she knew nary a soul in Denver, she said that she would make friends and get a job. "Doing What?" Pa chortled. "You don't have any skills or job experience."

That did it. Ma started packing. Pa called me out on the porch where he informed me in no uncertain terms that the stakes had gotten too high for us to lose. Losing a horse was one thing, but sacrificing Ma would be catastrophic. Of course, I had to agree, but all of my efforts came to naught when I tried to assure Pa that Ma would change her mind if Infernal Machine won the race. I had to win.

Having to win consumed me like my lusting after Doc Ruby's dancing girl, Fatima. The situation called for desperate plans. That is when I fell to my lowest level. I had to fix Grace's machine so it would lose come Sunday. The fear of getting caught trying to fix a wagered race hung over me like a burial pall draped over a casket. But, I had no choice. I became a student of sabotage, planning acts of covert mischief against my opponent.

All during that night, I couldn't sleep. My mind rummaged through various means of doing monkey business on Infernal Machine. It had to be something that would not be easily detected before the start of the race. A slow leak of air from a tire might work, but it would be unreliable. The drive belt from the engine to the rear wheel could be nipped a bit in several spots, making it fail during the race. I decided against that because a close inspection following the contest would reveal the deed. Another consideration was loosening a nut holding the front wheel or handlebars to the frame. I abandoned that idea—too dangerous. I didn't want to maim or kill my opponent.

By Saturday, we had ol' Spider in top shape. He could run a mile without faltering one bit and always had enough left to charge the finish line. My confidence had risen considerably, but not enough to be sure of winning against Grace's roaring motorcycle. My lack of confidence made fixing the race extremely important. The solution to my dilemma came to me the night before the contest while I was in our Relief Cottage. I was reading an article about internal combustion engines in the Casper Weekly Mail. The writer was discussing how to make an engine perform better at higher altitudes. He pointed out that an increased flow of air into the carburetor was required to provide enough oxygen for proper fuel combustion. Consequently, altitude lessened an engine's power unless the fuel to oxygen ratio was adjusted. That is when it dawned on me what I had to do. It seemed to be only three options. Fix the carburetor so it got too little air or too much fuel. The third option was to foul the ignition system. I had to find the Harper's Monthly from which I had torn the picture of an Orient-Aster and tacked on the wall.

I finally found it hidden among other magazines and newspapers, and preceded to read the original article, which described the Aster engine, a French copy of DeDion-Buton's ½ horsepower powerplant. *It was a small, light, high revving four-stroke single, and used battery-and-coil ignition, doing away with the troublesome hot-tube. Bore and stroke figures of 50 mm by 70 mm gave a displacement of 138 cc. A total loss lubrication system was employed to drip oil into the crankcase through a metering valve, which then sloshed around to lubricate and cool components before dumping it on the ground via a breather.* "That's it!" I yelled. "A goodly slug of blackstrap molasses into the oil reservoir should do the trick."

I sneaked back into the house and pilfered a jar of molasses from Ma's pantry. After slipping unseen out the back door, I headed for Sam Grace's home on the second story over his office. He kept his motorcycle chained to the hitching rail in front of the office. I was fortunate. The night was moonless, almost too dark for me to find my way down alleys and across vacant lots. I was certain he had left his office because there was a light in the upstairs window and the office was dark. I knelt down between his cycle and the wall so I wouldn't be seen by anyone riding by. I located the oil reservoir and unscrewed the cap. It was full of oil—no doubt having been toped off by Grace in preparation for the race next afternoon. That was a bit of bad luck. I didn't have anything to dip out any oil. My attention was drawn to White's Saloon about a block down the street. A bar had shot glasses—a lot of them. I hid Ma's molasses in my coat pocket and headed for the saloon.

I ordered a shot of Jack Daniels and slipped the glass into my pocket after downing its contents in one gulp. When I ordered my second round, Mister White ast me what happened to my glass. "Sorry," I said, trying to look real apologetic. "It slipped out of my hand and fell into the spittoon."

"Okay," he growled. "Fish that glass out of the spittoon afore y'get another drink."

I nodded my agreement and waited until he busied himself with serving another boozer. A spittoon ain't something y'want to stick your hand into. "Can I take it outside and dump out the glass?" I asked, bending down to pick it up.

"Yeah, go ahead."

Fortune had smiled on me once again. I ran down the street to perform my foul deed on Grace's pride and joy. I dipped oil from the reservoir, a shot-glassful at a time and poured them into the spittoon. When the reservoir was almost empty, I filled it with molasses and secured the cap. After emptying the spittoon into a garbage barrel behind Demorest's Café, I walked back to the saloon to return the filched items used to defile the Orient-Aster's engine. I set the spittoon on the floor next to the bar's foot rail and held out the shot glass to Mister White. He glanced at the glass tainted by oil and molasses and wagged his head. "Nobody can drink out of that again," he snarled.

"Yes, sir," I said, sidling toward the door.

I slept sound as a hibernating bear that night, confident that the race would be mine the next day. My dreams of leaving the Infernal Machine in a cloud of dust were interrupted the next morning when Pa slapped my rump and told me to get my fanny out of bed. It was the big day.

After breakfast, Ma got her nose out of joint again when Pa told her that he and I were too busy to go to church. She sniffed a couple of times, untied her apron, and stalked out of the kitchen, muttering something about our sinful ways and how we would get our just rewards. All the previous week, she had been miffed over what was printed in the last edition of the *Casper Weekly Mail*. Sam Grace had made certain there would be ample sweetening to the wagering pool by running a half-page ad. He bald-faced claimed that he'd cover any and all bets by anyone foolish enough to bet on my appaloosa. He even touted an unbiased holder of all bets—Clyde Hopkins, the bar tender at White's Saloon. I wouldn't trust ol' Clyde with ten cents, let alone a fist full of double eagles.

Besides publishing the ad, Sam convinced the folks down at the newspaper office to print an article covering the big event. Across the top of the front page was a blazing headline: RACE! RACE!! RACE!!! Below the headline was a double-column story about the contest. It went something like this: On Sunday next, Casper will be entertained by an unusual event—a mile-long race to determine which is the fastest, Tom Geiger's appaloosa or Sam Grace's motorcycle. The race will start one mile east of town and finish at the Fremont, Elkhorn and Missouri Valley Depot. Marshal Tigman will officiate the race, making certain the contestants only start the instant he fires his Colt into the air. In addition, he recruited Natrona County Sheriff Bill Conyers to supervise the finish line, a strip of red ribbon strung across the road between two poles. Since this will be a winner-take-all wager, either Geiger or Grace is going to be afoot following Sheriff Conyers' call at the end of the race. Sam Grace has promised an additional enticement for all racing fans. He will provide drinks on the house at White's Saloon after the spoils of the contest are distributed.

Well, I couldn't tell Ma or Pa why I wasn't worried about the outcome. Ol' Spider would still be in his stall out back in the pole shed on Monday morning. And I'd have me a nearly new Orient-Aster motorcycle parked on the back porch. Pa and I spent the remainder of the morning tending to ol' Spider. Pa groomed him from head to tail with a currycomb while I braided his mane and tied red ribbons at the end of each braid. After getting him all gussied up for the big event, I scrubbed down my saddle with saddle soap, and then buffed it until it looked brand new.

I reckon my rump-spotted steed was more nervous than I was because he kept snorting and wagging his head all morning. My usual pats on his shoulder and rump didn't seem to make any difference. Pa said that was a good sign. You need a horse with get up and go for any mile-long race.

Ma made her objections to the whole affair known at noon after she got home from church. Our usual Sunday dinner of roast beef, mashed potatoes, and buttered carrots wasn't to be. It was get whatever you want out of the cupboard and the well house out back. That is when I began to believe her threat to sashay on down to Denver.

I left the house at one o'clock astride the most adorned appaloosa that ever trotted down Center Street. Folks were already gathering around the depot when I passed by headed for the mile marker east of town. The resounding ovation we got was mixed with a lot of taunting remarks and a goodly number of boos. I waved real big and rode on out of town holding my head high like any confident jockey would do.

Marshal Tigman and a crowd met me at the mile marker. I'll give Tigman credit for keeping all of the unruly characters quiet while we waited for Sam Grace and his Infernal Machine to arrive. I began to worry about his showing up each time I flipped open my pocket watch to check the time. My biggest concern was whether all that molasses would foul his engine before he could reach the starting line. It was 5 minutes until 2 o'clock, the starting time of the race, when I heard the familiar drone of that Aster engine. He had that thing roaring full bore about a quarter mile down the road from us. He made a showy arrival by closing down the throttle and slamming on the brakes just about 50 yards from ol' Spider and me. I suppose his intention was to spook my trusty steed. Well it didn't work. My confidence soared as I reined ol' Spider away from Grace's Infernal Machine and settled him down with some soothing words and a lot of rein control.

"Time's a wastin'," Marshal Tigman said, pulling out his Colt. "Both of y'get at the starting line and get ready."

Both Grace and I eased our mounts up to the line. Grace revved his engine a couple of times and I leaned forward with my heels ready to nudge ol' Spider's belly. Tigman's Colt bellowed about that time and we were off. My charging steed leaped into a steady gallop right at the beginning like I had trained him to do. Infernal Machine roared past us, spewing smoke and dust into my face. I slapped ol' Spider's neck with the reins and yelled, "Get goin', hoss—HAH!"

Just then, my heart almost came to a stop. I could feel the fight goin' out of my struggling charger. His pace began to wane in spite of slapping reins and vocal encouragement. Then, my spirits soared when Infernal Machine sputtered, backfired, and died. Ol' Spider was down to a trot as we passed Grace who was trying to get life back into his motorcycle. But, my elation was soon squelched when ol' Spider stopped. I could feel him shuddering beneath my saddle as he snorted and heaved. I stepped out of the stirrup and jumped to the ground. "Come on, boy," I yelled, tugging on the reins. "You can make it. We can still beat Grace."

Just then, I heard a yahoo coming from Grace. Here he came pushing Infernal Machine as fast as he could. I tugged harder on the reins, but ol' Spider refused to budge. That's when Grace passed me, shoving that smoking contraption. "See y'at the depot," he yelled, waving goodbye.

About that time, Marshal Tigman's hoss came galloping toward me. "What's wrong with your Paloose?" Tigman yelled, reining his mount to a sliding stop.

"Don't know! He just quit."

I reckon Tigman knew more about fixing a race than I did. He checked ol' Spider over real quick. He slipped a finger into the left nostril, shook his head, and then eased his finger into the right nostril. "Your hoss has been corked," he said and began to swear words of condemnation upon Lawyer Grace.

"What's corked?"

"It's plugging one of a hoss's nostrils with a coned cork so's he's only getting half the air he needs."

My heart sank clear down to my knees about then. While I was fixing Grace's Infernal Machine, he or one of his cohorts was doing the same to my appaloosa. "Don't you worry none," the marshal said, stepping into his stirrup. "Anybody trying to fix a race that I'm in charge of is going to jail."

Well, what he said didn't stop my worrying for a moment. Molasses and corks came under the same category when it comes to fixing a race. If it hadn't been for Marshal Tigman and his deputy, the incensed crowds gathered at the starting and finish lines would have lynched ol' Sam and me. We doubled up astride their hosses and made a dash for Casper's crossbar hotel. The only thing that saved our necks from vigilante ropes were the scatterguns of Tigman and his deputy, and Ma who berated the mob of distraught bettors. While Sam and I cowered inside our cell, she waxed eloquent in front of the jail. She bellowed at the rabble with the zest of a hellfire-damnation preacher, calling down the wrath of the Almighty upon anyone laying a hand on her beloved son.

The grumbling mob began to disperse after Tigman assured them that justice would be done. He promised them that all of their bets would be returned and the court would attend to Sam and me as soon as a circuit judge arrived from Cheyenne.

Doc Stubben cured ol' Spider by removing the infamous cork, but nobody had the skill to repair Infernal Machine's seized-up engine. Sam was afoot for nearly a year while I saved up enough to buy him a new engine. Clyde Hopkins returned all of the bets and Sam Grace paid for drinks on the house, which sort of appeased the irate bettors. Ma didn't go to Denver; instead, she brought home-cooked meals to Grace and me while we did 30 days incarcerated together in the county jail. Her scathing oratory in front of the jail, apple pies and fried chicken caused Sam to drop his lawsuit against her and the ladies guild.

I don't reckon I'll ever forget the day Marshal Tigman unlocked our cell door and beckoned Sam and me to join him in his office. His parting words lacked any sympathy for our situation. "Mister Grace," he said, entering our releases in his record book. "Anymore trouble out of you and you'll be busting rocks down at the state prison instead of strutting around a courtroom."

Then he glanced at me over his reading spectacles. "As for you, young man, change your ways. Your ma may not be able to rescue your sorry fanny next time."

Buffalo Bill, Chung Lee and Me

Opportunity came knocking at my door in 1902. I'd had my fill of digging graves for the newly departed. It all came to a head early on a Saturday morning when I was driving our funeral coach out to Boot Hill. Pa and the Reverend Stowe were ahead of me, leading the funeral procession in Pa's brand new Studebaker buggy. Reposing in a shining ebony coffin inside our glass-sided coach was the recently departed Marshal Tigman. I had figured our aging town marshal would get smart enough to retire before some gun-slinging outlaw rode into town with robbery on his mind. The bank was next door to Tigman's office; consequently, everyone assumed nobody would dare pull a heist under those circumstances. The problem with that thinking was obvious to me—failing vision and hearing along with a palsied right hand had robbed him of being a competent lawman. He was no match for J. B. Packer who dared to rob the bank at 10 a.m. on the morning of February Third in 1902. I'll give Tigman credit for bravery, but that's all because he confronted an experienced shootist and bank robber when Packer stepped out of the bank. The marshal's dim vision and shaking hand was no match for the situation. He died without getting off a shot.

"Hold up there, sonny!" a commanding voice shouted just as I reined Pa's team of dapple-gray Percherons in front of the depot. When I turned to see who was yelling at me, a tall man with a white goatee and mustache, wearing a fringed buckskin jacket and a ten-gallon white hat sauntered through the depot doorway. I recognized him right away. "Whoa!" I yelled and reached down to shake his hand. "Yes, sir, Mister Cody."

"Who might y'be burying?"

"Marshal Tigman."

"Harley—Harley Tigman?"

"Yes, sir."

"How'd he die?"

"J. B. Packer kilt him while holding up the bank last Tuesday."

"Well, I declare, mind if I ride along with you? Harley and I go back a lot o' years."

"You're welcome—climb aboard."

William F. "Buffalo Bill" Cody was something to behold. I'd been reading about him for a lot of years. We had several of Ned Buntline's novels about how Buffalo Bill nearly tamed the West by himself. One of them told how he kilt ol' Chief Yellow Hand and scalped him so's he could avenge the massacre of Custer and the 7th Cavalry. But the main thing I remember about Buffalo Bill is how he handled his big white hoss during every performance of The Wild West Show. He rode with flair, like some medieval knight getting ready for a jousting party.

On the way to boot hill, Buffalo Bill and I got acquainted. I was real impressed by how friendly he was. He first told me how he and Marshal Tigman used to ride together back in the early days. They had been riders for the Pony Express when both of them were only 14 years old. Later, during the Civil War, they were scouts for the Seventh Kansas Cavalry. Following the War, Buffalo Bill earned his nickname by killing over 4,000 buffalo in just 18 months. And Harley Tigman tried his hand at robbing stages, but changed his ways after spending two years in the Fort Leavenworth prisoner stockade. "Reckon ol' Harley picked the wrong stage that was carrying the garrison payroll for Fort Kearney, Nebraska," Buffalo Bill said, spat, and wiped brown tobacco-stained spittle from his goatee.

That bit of news made my heart soar. If I had only known about it when the marshal was heckling me about my awkward ways. "Talk about being stupid," I muttered and busted into a crescendo of heehaws.

"About as stupid as stupid gets," Cody said and then chuckled at the memory. "The troopers ridin' out of Fort Kearney took offense at his oversight. Yes, sir, they caught him before he could spend a single dollar of their pay."

None of Casper's folks apparently knew about Tigman's indiscretions as a young man—at least nobody ever mentioned anything about them. He was highly respected for being an effective lawman. Ma was especially fond of him, mostly for his discouraging remarks about my becoming a U. S. marshal. I hated him for doing that to me. Now, I was going to realize a smidgeon of soul salve for my wounded spirit. Yes, sir, Ma was going to hear the plain truth about her hero. I must have been smirking a lot about then, because Cody grasped my arm. "This is just twixt us," he said, gripping harder with each word he uttered. "No need t'tarnish a good man's memory."

"Yes, sir," I croaked and snapped the reins a couple of times. "Hah! Get moving, hosses."

The rein snapping and yelling weren't really necessary. It was just a means of closing our conversation about my departed passenger.

Cody loosened his grip. "Y'handle your team like a real teamster."

"I reckon, but ain't no future in driving this rig and digging graves."

"What about the business when your pa retires?"

"I ain't going to be a mortician—can't stand formaldehyde."

"You could hire an embalmer."

"Maybe, but burying dead folks ain't for me."

"Hmm." Cody knuckled his mustache and fell silent, apparently pondering what I'd said.

Neither of us spoke until we reached Boot Hill. I was reining the hosses through the gate when Bill slapped my shoulder. "If you'd like to join my Wild West Show, I could use another man good with horses."

I yanked back on the reins. "Whoa!" At last, opportunity had come my way. It was sort of like what happens to a dying man when his experiences go flashing in front of his eyes. My past even bored me again as it zipped by. There wasn't any need to ponder his offer. I was willing to do just about any task to escape the humdrum life of a mortician's son in Casper, Wyoming. My hand shot out like a drunk reaching for a shot of whiskey. "Put her there—when do I start?"

"Right away—soon as we get Harley properly planted."

"Whoopee!" I yelled and snapped the reins. "Time's wastin', hosses."

After we shoveled the last spade full of dirt onto Marshal Tigman's place of eternal repose, Bill and I drove the coach back to the storage shed. Cody was true to his word. He even helped me explain my decision to Pa and Ma. Ma was properly impressed by the presence of Buffalo Bill in her parlor. It was something she would brag about to the ladies guild for a lot of years. And the news about me being hired to work in his Wild West Show was an embellishment beyond her wildest dreams. Pa was less impressed. That's because he would have to hire someone to perform my menial tasks.

I'll not soon forget the waving crowd at the depot when Bill and I boarded the train. I can still hear the cheering of his admirers above the screeching locomotive whistle as the engineer pushed open the throttle. When the train gathered speed, the click-clack of steel wheels racing along the rails assured me that I was embarking upon a new era. I was going to be a showman—maybe even have a Wild West show of my own some day. Bill pulled out a pocket humidor, flipped it open and offered me a Havana cheroot. "Reckon it's time for a little celebration, eh Tom?"

"Reckon so," I said, bit off the tip of the cigar and spat it on the floor. Cody helped himself to a stogie and swiped a match to life across his britches. After taking several puffs, we swallowed a couple of swigs of whiskey from his sterling silver pocket flask. Now that's living—smoking and drinking with one of the most famous men in the world. Yes, sir, I was basking in my dreams of fame and fortune.

We arrived in Denver about nine o'clock that night where The Wild West Show was being prepared for a summer tour across the eastern states. It was scheduled to wind up in

New York where the entire show would be loaded onto a ship bound for Europe.

I hadn't realized how large his show was before Bill took me out to the assembling grounds where everything was being loaded onto railroad cars. The show was going to travel in two sections. Most of the performers and Buffalo Bill would ride in passenger cars making up the first section. All of the equipment and stock under the care of some Indians and roustabouts were in freight or on flatbed cars in the second section. Each section of the tour required its own big steam locomotive.

Several days went by before the two trains were ready to leave Denver. During that delay, I got acquainted with several of the show folks. There were hundreds of performers required to enact the individual extravaganzas. Some of the most popular shows were the Buffalo Hunt, Great Train Robbery, Indian War Battle Reenactment, and the Grand Finale—The Attack on the Burning Cabin.

*　*　*

Both trains pulled out of Denver early on April Fool's Day. After Bill told me to stow my belongings under a spare bunk in his private Pullman car, I began to strut my stuff. There I was, Tom Geiger, hobnobbing with the one and only Buffalo Bill. I'd never seen, let alone ridden in a genuine Pullman car. And it wasn't any old ordinary car. It was fancied up with all of the accoutrements required for living high on the rails. There was a bar with more bottles in its cabinet than White's Saloon had back in Casper. And Bill was real free with the booze in those bottles. Right away, he ast me what brand I preferred for sipping. I leaned back in my chair, crossed my boots, stuck my thumbs in the armholes of my leather vest and assumed the nonchalant pose of a well-heeled traveler. "Gentleman Jack suits my fancy just fine."

That's when I discovered Bill's craving for sour mash likker. "Ah, yes, nobody does it better than Mister Jack Daniel."

While filling two shot glasses, he continued, waxing eloquent as a bible-thumping preacher while extolling the virtues of Jack Daniel's whiskey. He claimed that its unique amber color and smoky flavor made it the preferred beverage of gentlemen around the world. I learned all about distilling and drinking booze that morning while Bill and I sipped and sipped. I also learned how too much of it could bite like a tiger and sting like a hornet. The puking and thumping headache turned me against sipping for quite a spell.

*   *   *

Bill had posters all over the walls of his private car. Some of them were of Sitting Bull, dressed up in his feathered bonnet; Annie Oakley, whose real name was Phoebe Ann Moses; Texas Jack, a cowboy wearing a ten-gallon hat and fleecy chaps, and Pablo Alvarez, a Mexican vaquero attired in a sombrero and silver-studded vest. I really took a liking to the pictures of Annie Oakley. One showed her shooting off the end of a cigar clinched between the teeth of a German Kaiser. Now, that took a lot of guts on both their parts. I surely did want to meet her, but she had left the show the year before in 1901.

Our train made good time. We were about four miles ahead of the second train during most of the trip. We had been travelling for a couple of days when Bill slapped me on the behind and told me t'wake up. "What's happening?" I muttered, rubbing the sleep out of my eyes.

"We're stopping. All of the horses and stock have t'be unloaded."

"Why?"

"Got a show t'put on in a couple of days."

I looked out the window. We were parked on a rail siding. All kind of commotions was going on—Indians and roustabouts were unloading horses, mules and other stock. "Where are we?"

"Fort Worth, Texas."

It took us two days to get the show ready t'go. All around the grounds where we were setting up everything, the show folks were busy as a pond full of beavers building a dam. Wagons for the races had to be assembled. Tiered seats for spectators were put together around the various arenas. I hadn't seen that much stuff going on in my entire life. The most important thing I learned was to stay out of everybody's way. A

Texas longhorn, elk, or an enraged buffalo could gore you real easy if you didn't watch your backside. My assignment was to take care of Bill's white stallion. I washed and curried him until he was shining bright as a new dollar. Then I had to tidy up his silver studded saddle, making sure the leather was properly cleaned with a goodly amount of saddle soap and elbow grease. I decided it would be to my advantage if I slept next to the stud's stall just to make certain nothing happened. There couldn't be anything done if some filly in heat was to get upwind from him, but it seemed to be the right thing to do. Fortunately, the night passed without incident.

The morning of the show dawned clear and bright. Chung Lee, Bill's private chef, brought me bacon, scrambled eggs, biscuits, and an ample portion of sorghum molasses to sop biscuits in. Chung was a quaint little feller—Chinese y'know. He didn't care much for American cooking, but fortunately for me, Bill didn't want bird nest soup or the likes thereof for breakfast. Chung had been with Bill for a lot of years and he was real knowledgeable about his boss's likes and dislikes. Consequently, the Chinese dishes that he served were only the one's that Bill fancied, such as egg rolls and chow mien. "Thanks," I said to Chung as he set my platter on a bale of hay. "When does the show start?"

"Boss want horse thirty minute before show begin two-clock."

I winked knowingly and nodded at Chung. "Y'bet, I'll have him saddled, bridled and ready t'go."

I fed alfalfa hay and oats to the stud and fetched a bucket of water for him from the tank car. We got along just fine until it came to getting him bridled and saddled. When I threw a saddle blanket over his back, he began to roll his eyes and toss his head. Then he began to prance around like one of those Austrian war stallions I'd read about. That's when I decided to stay clear of his hind end—didn't want to get a hoof slammed into my gut. After about twenty minutes of sidestepping and sweet-talking, I managed to get him saddled and bridled. Once that was accomplished, I opened the stall gate and led him toward Buffalo Bill's tent.

I could feel excitement in the air.   The crowd was gathering in the great arena.   The band was practicing in a pavilion next to Buffalo Bill's tent where he dressed up in his show regalia.   Across on the other side of the arena, a calliope was getting up a full head of steam in preparation for the grand opening.   Soon, the show would begin when Buffalo Bill would lead the parade of flags astride his white stallion.   The moment was intense.   My heart pounded.   I didn't realize it at the time, but stage fever had set in.   I didn't want to be a wrangler in charge of a hoss.   I was a born entertainer that had to perform. My better senses were overcome by the moment.   Before thinking, I stepped into the stirrup and swung a leg over Buffalo Bill's stallion.   It was a humongous mistake.   The stud suddenly began to prance and canter around in a circle.   "Whoa—whoa," I yelled, yanking back on the reins.   It didn't help.   I about decided to get off when he stopped dead in his tracks, swished his tail and began to prance backwards.

Just then, four mounted riders bearing flags of the United States, Great Britain, Canada and Mexico came galloping toward the arena gate.   The stud apparently figured Buffalo Bill was sitting in his saddle, because he leapt into a gallop towards the four horsemen.   All of my screeching and rein yanking had no effect on his determination.   I was headed for the grand opening—the presentation of flags that preceded the parade of performers in Cody's theatrical troupe.   And it was a nearly endless parade of the Congress of Rough Riders, which included American cavalrymen, German Cuirassiers, Mexican vaqueros, Cossacks, Arabs, Cubans, cowboys and Indians.   Stagecoaches, covered wagons, Indian ponies pulling travois, and trick riders standing atop bareback ponies followed them.

"Whoa up, y'damn knot head," I shrieked and pulled hard as I could on the reins.   The stud, racing to join the flag bearers, suddenly came to a sliding halt.   The stop was too quick for me to stay in the saddle.   I sailed over his head and landed spread-eagled in Fort Worth dust.   I reckon I was too addled to understand all of Cody's profanity as he leaped on his stallion and galloped into the arena.   But I was certain about his displeasure with my antics.

While I was recovering in Cody's tent, Chung let me know where I had erred. He explained in Chinese accented English how Buffalo Bill had trained his stallion to perform. Most of his commands for specific actions were in the form of leg and knee pressures, along with neck reining and vocal directions. Cody had also taught him to rear up or come to a sliding halt by shifting his weight in the saddle. I reckon my bouncing posterior had conveyed the wrong message.

When the show was over, Bill rode the stallion back to his tent where I was awaiting my fate. He bolted through the doorway, yanked off his white gauntlets and slammed them on the cot where I was cringing. "Who said you could ride my hoss?"

My jaw was locked from fear and embarrassment. I stared at the dirt floor, trying to conjure up some excuse that might get me out of my mess.

"Well—I'm wantin' an answer."

"Nobody!"

"You damn near ruined my grand opener. That stallion was so upset by what you did, I couldn't do anything with him."

I finally got up enough gumption to look at him. I've seen anger in Pa and Ma's eyes before, but it wasn't anything like what I saw in Buffalo Bill's eyes. "Sorry, sir, I didn't mean t'harm."

He stood there gazing at my shaky countenance and wagged his head. Finally, he took off his ten-gallon hat and tossed it to Chung who had stuck his head through the doorway. Chung must have figured Cody was going to do me in or thrash my posterior. Bill sat down on the cot beside me. We sat there for what seemed like an eternity without speaking. I pondered my screw-up while contemplating the dirt floor. It seemed that if anything could go haywire, it would.

Our face-off ended when Chung handed each one of us a shot glass filled with Jack Daniel's. "You fellow drink—forget—okay?"

The next thing I knew, Bill draped an arm around my shoulders and lifted his glass. "A horseman you are not, Tom, but there's got to be something you can do."

I touched his glass with mine. He slapped my shoulder and we downed our booze. From that moment on, Bill never mentioned my blunder and I sure didn't bring it up.

* * *

The show ran for three days before we packed up the trains and pulled out of Fort Worth. Our next show would be in Atlanta, Georgia. While travelling across Texas, Louisiana and Alabama, I brooded over telling Cody my decision. I wanted to be a trick-shot artist, one that could equal the feats of Annie Oakley. She was one of the most famous performers in the Wild West Show, being known around the world as "Little Sure Shot". Buffalo Bill bragged about how well she could ride a hoss and shoot at the same time. I yearned to gain notoriety doing the same things. That's when I decided to get some first rate tutoring in the fine art of marksmanship. With the exception of Cody's stallion, I figured I could ride a hoss as good as anybody. I wasn't too fast on the draw with a six-gun, but my abilities with a rifle could be as good as hers. If a snip of a gal like Annie could split a cigar at 20 paces, my talents could do the same— maybe even better. Chung had been with the show for a lot of years, so I decided to ast him who could teach me to shoot like Annie.

"Chung Lee," he replied.

"You—Chung?"

"Me! I teach Annie."

I was flabbergasted. Annie Oakley had been trained to be the world's best trick-shot artist by a Chinese cook? "Okay, when can we start?"

"We go now—I get two rifle."

I glanced out of the Pullman window at telegraph poles racing by. "Reckon we'd better wait till the train stops?"

"We shoot now," he said, pointing toward the back of the car.

Chung opened Bill's gun cabinet, pulled out two carbines and a box of ammunition. Then he shuffled behind the bar and began to rummage through the trash barrel. After handing me several empty whiskey bottles, he retrieved some shot glasses from the bar and dropped them into his pocket.

We opened the Pullman door and stepped out onto the rear platform. Chung handed me a carbine and a cartridge. "You know how load?"

I frowned and looked down at his moon-shaped face and inquiring eyes staring up at me. "Of course I do—I've hunted antelope, deer and elk with my pa."

"That good. You load rifle. Don't shoot till I say to."

I grasped the lever, threw open the action, slipped a cartridge into the receiver and slammed the lever closed. I glanced at Chung to see whether he was intimidated by the quickness of my actions. He didn't seem impressed. "Okay, I shoot first," he said, loading his carbine. "Chung show how."

Without hesitating, he yelled for me to throw a whiskey bottle high as I could, which I did with gusto. When the bottle reached the highest point of its flight, Chung flipped the carbine to his shoulder and fired. The bottle exploded into a shower of shards. I was impressed.

He handed me a shot glass—I gave it the old heave ho and his bullet blew it to smithereens. "Wow, that's some shootin'."

"Okay—I throw whiskey bottle—you shoot."

I tried to copy his feat, but the bottle didn't bust until it hit the ground. "Damn it, I missed."

"No! No! You shoot when bottle reach apogee."

"Apo … what?

"Apogee—at point bottle stop go up and start down. Okay?"

"Oh, I see."

Chung let the second bottle fly with all the power his five-foot-one could muster. I yanked the carbine to my shoulder and pulled the trigger the moment it reached its apogee. The bottle disintegrated as my bullet tore through Jack Daniel's label. "Whoopee," I yelled and began to dance a jig. "I did it. I did it."

"Not so fast—you shoot shot glass. Okay?"

Chung threw up four shot glasses before I managed to bust one. However, I got two out of the next three. Chung's face broke into a wide toothy grin. "Chung good teacher—you learn more tomorrow."

We practiced many different shots during the following couple of weeks. He taught me how to shoot from an assortment of positions, even at a target behind me using a mirror to sight with over my shoulder. My skill got so good that it seemed certain Buffalo Bill would ask me to perform—maybe before the show closed in Atlanta. Chung Lee wasn't as excited about my prowess with a carbine, but we continued to practice every moment he could spare.

* * *

Cody assigned me to help tend horses, mules, longhorns, buffalo, elk, and a couple of llamas. He wouldn't listen to my pleadings about performing trick shots. It must have been my reckless handling of his stallion that convinced him to be wary of my accomplishments. So, feeding, watering, and pampering animals, and shoveling manure became my lot. You would be amazed at how much manure all of those critters can manufacture. And there is the problem of what to do with that much waste. Cody wasn't a dumbo when it came to business. When I ast him what we were going to do with all of it, he gave me a typical Cody response. "Why pay to dispose of manure when you can sell it?"

I don't know what he charged for a load of animal muck. It was just my job to help shovel it into customers' wagons. It seems that elk, buffalo and llama poop was valued above the rest. At least, it appeared that way to me, because we had to keep it in separate piles. To my annoyance, I became known as the fertilizer king of Cody's Wild West Show.

It didn't take long for me to make up my mind. The life of a manure handler wasn't for me. I'd sooner dig graves and drive a funeral coach in Casper, Wyoming. When we loaded up to leave Atlanta for Danville, Virginia, I decided that either I was going to be a performer or my carcass was heading back to Casper. That's when I had a little conversation with the high and mighty maestro of the Wild West Show. It was after an evening of idle conversation and a supper of egg rolls and chicken chow mien that I cleared the tremor out of my throat and spoke my piece to Bill. "These calluses are on the hands of a manure scooper," I said, holding them up for him to see. "I ain't going to scoop another shovel full of animal muck. No, sir, not one more scoop of crap."

Cody peered at me with a bit of astonishment imprinted on his rugged features. He sort of mulled over what I'd said, and then pushed my hands away. "Tom," he said with a solemn tone in his voice. "Just what can you do to earn your keep?"

"Trick shootin'."

"You—perform trick shots?"

"Yes, sir. I've hinted at it a lot of times, but you haven't heard me."

"When did you learn trick shootin'?"

"Chung's been teachin' me—just ast him."

"I will." He picked up the little hand bell he used to summon Chung Lee and rang it with more vigor than usual.

Chung shuffled into the dinning area. "Yes, Mister Cody—what you need?"

Tom says you have been teachin' him to do trick shooting."

Chung nodded. "That correct."

"Is he any good?"

Chung glanced my way and cleared his throat. "He okay. Not like Annie—just okay."

Bill bowed his head and studied the remnants of chow mien on his plate. I waited for his comment, which seemed like a lot of minutes. He turned toward me. "I'm willin' to see what you can do in the morning before we pull out for Virginia."

Early the following morning, Bill, Chung and I walked down into a ravine next to the railroad tracks. My big moment had arrived. I was going to be a Wild West trick-shot artist. I managed to break all of the bottles and glasses that Chung threw skyward. Then I demonstrated rapid firing from the hip. I levered and fired ten rounds in brisk succession, making a tin can dance down the ravine. My big finish was using a hand-held mirror to shoot at a target located twenty paces behind me. The target would be the dollop of ashes on the tip of a large Cuban cigar being held in Chung's outstretched hand. This required me to lay the rifle back across my left shoulder and aim at the cigar using one of Annie Oakley's mirrors. I wasn't worried about hurting Chung, because we had pulled it off several times before. Bill wasn't quite as confident. While I was getting set, and Chung was lighting a cigar, he asked Chung if he was sure about going ahead.

"Not worry—Tom okay."

"You're sure?"

"Tom okay—Chung okay."

I leveled the rifle across my shoulder and got a good view of the smoldering cigar in the mirror. I'll say this for Chung; his hand was steady, no wavering at all. The only problem I encountered was a swarm of flies that kept buzzing around my head. One lit on my nose and began to rummage around for whatever tidbits a fly desires. I tried to dislodge the pesky critter with facial contortions but it didn't respond. Finally, I gritted my teeth, aimed and fired. The dollop of ash on the tip of the cigar disintegrated. Chung yelled, "Whoopee—I still got hand."

My biggest reward was when Cody slapped me on the back. "That's quite a demonstration, Tom. Chung has taught you well."

"Y'want me to perform?"

"Sure—we'll talk about it on the train.

* * *

During our trek toward Danville, Virginia, Cody and I got everything ironed out concerning my new trick-shooting performance. He didn't want me to do any riding and shooting right off. Instead, I was to put on my demonstration in the great arena between the Buffalo Hunt and the Great Train Robbery. As an added guarantee that my introduction would go well, he came up with what I considered to be a goofy idea. Chung Lee was going to dress up just like Annie Oakley. His small stature, a brunette wig of spiraling curls, and Annie's western attire, which Cody kept in a theatrical trunk she had left behind, gave him a striking resemblance to the petite sharpshooter. Part of the act was for Annie Oakley to introduce me, Tom Geiger, trick-shot artist hailing from Casper, Wyoming, to the crowd. The introduction was intended to pass Annie's mantle of excellence on to me, her successor. The entire idea bothered me a lot. How was Chung Lee going to fool anybody about being Annie Oakley? Every time we practiced his intro, I couldn't contain myself. "Ladies! Gentlemen! I, Annie Oakley—best shot world—retire. This fellow—Tom Geiger—takes place. I teach. Shoot good. Welcome!"

All of the coaching that Bill and I tried never changed his speech. Consequently, I managed to convince Cody that it wasn't going to work. The crowd would be laughing so hard they couldn't watch my act through their tears. So, he scratched Chung from the performance. It was all up to me. Buffalo Bill Cody would make my introduction.

Our train rolled into North Carolina that night about an hour after dark. We had just finished eating one of Chung's culinary creations; Peking duck with orange sauce, when our engineer, ol' Bob Pierce, pulled us into Lexington. There was a freight train on the siding; apparently waiting for us to clear the tracks so its engineer could proceed westward. I reckon both engineers got their signals mixed up, because the westbound train pulled out onto the main tracks after our eastbound train passed. Ol' Bob slammed on our brakes but it took us a quarter mile to stop. By that time, the westbound freight was barreling out of town headed for an unpleasant encounter with the second show train coming behind us. It was too late—there wasn't anything that could be done to warn either engineer of their rapidly converging locomotives.

Ol' Bob Pierce started backing our train real slow down the track toward whatever catastrophe was going to happen. It seemed like we never were going to get to the wreckage that was bound to be waiting for us. Several roustabouts on the second train heard us coming and managed to get two lanterns lit. When Ol' Bob saw them waving those lanterns, he slammed on the brakes. We all jumped off the train to do whatever we could for the injured folks.

It was a mess. The trains had met head on about four miles out of Lexington near Linwood. Just before the collision, the engineers and firemen of both trains survived by leaping into a swamp on the north side of the tracks. Since all of the cars on both trains were made of wood, they shattered into piles of splintered rubble. Most of the wreckage wound up in Swearing Creek, which runs along the south side of the track. Nary a soul got kilt, but some of our show folks got banged up. The stock didn't fare as well. A lot of horses, cattle, buffalo, several elk and both llamas died in the wreck. Some horses had to be shot—others were given to the local folks. Buffalo Bill's big white stallion got kilt outright, as well as two stallions that the Queen of England had given him. The show was in shambles and out of business.

Cody was real generous with all us show folks, paying for all of our needs until the show train could be sent on its way back home. We left after several days, but he stayed in Linwood until the Southern Railway Company cleared up the mess.

While we were headed west toward Colorado and Wyoming, I brooded over my situation. I should have been used to failure, having enjoyed a steady diet of it since childhood. I could have been a world-renowned shootist if it hadn't been for that stupid freight-train engineer. I might have performed for the Queen of England, the Tsar of Russia, and the Kaiser of Germany. The folks in Casper, especially Ma and Pa, would have all been waiting at the depot when I returned. The local band would be playing and the mayor would hand me the keys to Casper. *Casper Weekly Mail* headlines would announce the return of Casper's favorite son—WELCOME HOME TOM GEIGER!! ENTERTAINER OF ROYALTY!!! WORLD RENOWNED TRICK-SHOT ARTIST!!!!

The pain of blistered palms and eye-smarting fumes of formaldehyde wafted from the recesses of my mind. It was a disconcerting reminder of what actually awaited me upon my arrival back home. I decided Tom Geiger was never going to set foot in Casper, Wyoming again. No, sir, I wasn't going to dig another grave, nor uncork another bottle of formaldehyde. It was at that moment when providence came tapping. The conductor sauntered down the isle, toting several copies of *The Denver Post*. I pulled a nickel out of my vest pocket and held up my hand to get his attention. "How 'bout one of them papers?"

He tossed me one, grabbed my nickel and ambled on down the isle. The first article I noticed was about the upcoming sixth annual Cheyenne Frontier Days Rodeo. It was going to be the greatest rodeo of all. I sat there looking out the window while pondering my future. I could ride a bronco, do trick shooting, or about anything else needed for a first class rodeo exhibition. "Oh, conductor," I yelled. "I won't be getting off until we reach Cheyenne."

Bill Pickett and Friend

Ralph Doubleday wasn't the first professional photographer to take pictures of heart-stopping action in a rodeo arena. I was.

It all started in May of 1903 during the special Frontier Days Rodeo put on to entertain President Teddy Roosevelt in Cheyenne, Wyoming. While returning from Virginia following the big wreck of Buffalo Bill's Wild West Show train near Danville, I decided to become a rodeo performer—you know, riding broncs, roping steers, and doing a little trick shooting on the side. Well, it didn't quite work out like I'd expected. The biggest letdown was not getting paid to perform. It seems the folks who started the granddaddy of all rodeos weren't too keen about paying wages or winnings. It was a slight oversight on their part. I'd grown quite fond of having a bed and enough grub t'keep some fat on my skinny frame. I had to get a job. For the time being, I'd leave riding broncs and roping steers to real cowboys who rode for big spreads like the Pitchfork up near Meeteetse, Wyoming.

The memory of my first week in Cheyenne isn't too thrilling. My bed was a cast-iron bench on the loading platform of the Union Pacific Railroad station. Grub was hard to come by. Starvation would have been my lot if it hadn't been for the generosity of station agent Cal Leghorn. Ol' Cal let me eat on the cuff in the Depot Café and Lounge until I found a job. Of course, I had to contribute by busing tables and washing dishes. That temporary arrangement ended a week after I stepped off the train in Cheyenne. That's when Ezra Pheipher took a picture of me while I was asleep on my iron bench. He must have thought my half-open eyes, gaping mouth and shabby attire would illustrate his article on vagrancy scheduled for publication in *The Cheyenne Sun-Leader*.

Ezra had one of those detective cameras that looked like a revolver, a bit risky to use in a rowdy frontier town. Some drunk, gun-toting cowboy might slap leather, mistaking such a device for a genuine hogleg. But, I reckon he wasn't in any danger when shooting pictures of a sleeping vagrant like me. I wouldn't have waked up if it hadn't been for all the guffaws echoing up and down the station platform. Passengers boarding the train bound for San Francisco were quite amused by his strange camera and grubby subject.

"Got no money," I yelled, raising my hands.

He held out his contraption for me to inspect. "Relax, sonny. This is a camera."

Being unconvinced of what he claimed, I looked over the strange device while he explained how it worked. Behind the barrel, which contained the lens, several tiny photographic plates were fitted into a revolving cylinder. One plate moved into position and cocked the shutter each time the cylinder was rotated. A photo was then taken by pulling the trigger just like firing a Colt revolver.

Ol' Ezra had emigrated from England where he was a photographer and reporter for a London newspaper. The folks in Cheyenne weren't accustomed to any man who toted a collapsible umbrella, wore a black bowler hat, and had a monocle dangling from a black ribbon pinned to his vest. And there was his peculiar accent punctuated with an occasional oath, such as: "Blimey." "Right old chap." "Bloody well." I reckon his unusual attire and British mannerisms were probably what kept him from getting gunshot whenever he whipped out his hogleg camera.

Ezra and I hit it off—after I recovered from being confronted by a weird photographer, that is. He seemed impressed by my interest in picture taking. After answering a steady stream of questions, he invited me to accompany him to *The Cheyenne Sun-Leader* offices. There, he showed me how to develop exposed plates in the darkroom. The place stunk a little like Pa's embalming room, but the developing chemicals didn't smart my eyes like formaldehyde. I decided this was something I could excel at. I envisioned my byline under most of the pictures published in the newspaper. And there would be many awards for artistic accomplishments coming my way. Yes, things were beginning to look up.

We left the darkroom and walked down a hallway to his office where hundreds of pictures were pinned to the wall. He laid the hogleg camera on his desk and gestured for me to take a chair. When he sat behind the desk, he had a puzzled expression—you know, sort of a quizzical look in his eyes. "I must apologize for my negligence," he said, reaching across the desk. "My name is Ezra Pheipher."

I shook his hand and leaned back in my chair. "Mighty proud t'meetcha, Mister Pheipher. I'm Tom Geiger."

"Ah, yes, Tom. Would you join me in a toddy?"

I had no idea what a toddy might be—but why not? "Reckon I would."

While sipping a yucky mixture of brandy, hot water, sugar and potent spices, I pondered Ezra's pictures. The brandy and some innate brashness loosened my tongue. "How 'bout me learning to take pictures?"

Ezra popped the monocle over his right eye and gave me a once over like a fox ogling a rabbit's burrow. "Blimey, old chap, any newspaper experience?"

"Nope."

"None?"

"Well—I used to drop into the *Casper Weekly Mail* to watch Herb Smith set type."

"Can you set type?"

"Reckon I could. Ain't much to it."

"How many lines can you set in a minute?"

"Don't rightly know—never tried."

Ezra's forehead furrowed as he contemplated my nervous composure. He didn't have to say anything. His thinking was obvious.

"I could learn."

"Yes, you might, but there won't be much pay to start."

Anything would be an improvement over sleeping on a cast-iron bench, eating leftover grub and surviving without a place to take a bath or wash clothes. "Don't need much—just enough for room and board."

Ezra pursed his lips and stared into the distance. Finally, he opened his desk drawer, pulled out a business card and penned something on the back of it. "All right," he said, handing it to me. "My card will admit you to the Cheyenne Club where you will be provided room and board." He then pulled a gold double eagle from his pocket and flipped it to me. "Get yourself a new wardrobe at Harrison's Store."

I fondled that coin for quite a spell before I could respond. "Y'mean, I'm hired?"

"You'll be my assistant provided you learn to be a photographer within six weeks."

* * *

As it turned out, my darkroom performance was a failure. The fumes emitted by photographic developer and fixer slithered up my nose, which provoked copious nasal secretions and frequent bouts of sneezing. Phlegm-splattered plates don't produce acceptable pictures. If it hadn't been for George Eastman's new box camera, I would have been sleeping on an iron bench again. Ezra ordered one for me. It arrived loaded with a hundred-exposure roll of film. Since we couldn't develop their film, the camera had to be returned to the Kodak folks in Denver. They would process my pictures, reload the camera with another roll of film, and return the camera and pictures to me.

I was on my first roll of film when President Teddy Roosevelt stepped off the train. Ezra had taken to his bed the day before with a fierce attack of gout. So, the day belonged to ol' Teddy and me. Besides getting to meet the President of the United States, I was going to document an historical event. He was greeted by a crowd of folks, most all of them bent on getting their pictures taken while shaking his hand. Their desires turned good fortune in my direction. I held up my camera and yelled to get Teddy's attention. "Here, Sir, Tom Geiger from *The Cheyenne Sun-Leader*."

The crowd stepped aside sort of like the Red Sea opening up for ol' Moses and his throng. I advanced toward the

President with my camera at the ready just like stalking a wily elk. He tilted back his head and showed me the widest spread of teeth I'd ever seen. That was when the crowd began to surge back together. I felt like Pharaoh's army being caught between two walls of water just as the last Hebrew climbed out of the seabed onto dry land. That's when Teddy rescued my newly chosen profession for me. "Move aside, folks," he bellowed. "Let Mister Geiger through."

"Thank you, Mister President," I said, framing his rotund figure in my viewfinder.

"You're quite welcome, young man. Take your time."

The crowd remained stock-still as my clicking shutter captured several shots of the President's lively expressions. After getting enough exposures to satisfy Ezra, I spoke my appreciations. He proved his reputation for being the best politician of the day by asking me to let his secretary use my Kodak to take a picture of us shaking hands. After that, I would have voted for him to be Emperor of the world.

* * *

I was waxing in heady success the following morning. Ezra was still laid up with a throbbing big toe. The assignment was mine to photograph the special Frontier Days Rodeo being put on for Roosevelt. With the strap of my camera slung over my shoulder and a *PRESS* card pinned to the crown of my new Stetson, I boarded the horse-drawn Cheyenne trolley. "Howdy," I said, taking a seat next to a black cowboy wearing sheepskin chaps, a buckskin vest, manure-encrusted boots and a "sugarloaf" hat.

He knuckled his bewhiskered chin while eying my press card. "Howdy, sonny, y'headin' for the ro-de-oh?"

I thrust out my chest and pointed at the card pinned to my hat. "I'm Tom Geiger. I'm a photographer for the *Sun-Leader.*"

"I'm Bill Pickett," he said reaching for my hand. "I'm a bronc buster and bulldogger."

"What's a bulldogger?"

Pickett unlatched his carpetbag and pulled out a Midland, Texas newspaper. "Read this," he said, pointing at a front-page headline. *Bill Pickettt, Local "Negro" Cowboy, Throws Wild Steer by the Nose with his Teeth! Bill Pickett who has purportedly developed a new method of wrestling a steer to the ground entertained folks attending the fair yesterday. Pickett, astride his pony, Spradley, pursued a steer across the rodeo arena until he was able to leap on the steer, grasp its horns, twist its neck and sink his teeth into its lip. Pickett hung on like a persistent bulldog until the unfortunate steer collapsed to the ground. Pickett claims that he got the idea from reading an account of how bulldogs were used for amusement in the Elizabethan era to fight bulls. The bulldogs would grasp the bull's snout with their powerful jaws and hang on until the stricken animal collapsed. Pickett said he first used this method to subdue a steer that refused to go into a corral.*

"Are you going to bulldog a steer today?" I asked, handing the paper back to him.

"Well, I was, but Curly Bill Johnson and I got into a fight last night at the Hitchin' Post Saloon. I smashed his nose and he knocked out a couple of my front teeth."

That's when inspiration jumped on me like a hawk swooping down to catch a chicken. "How 'bout me?"

Pickett gave me the once-over again. He had skeptical written all over his face. "What?"

"Got all my teeth," I said and opened my mouth to demonstrate a full set of choppers.

"Y'got good teeth, but if you think you can take a steer down with 'em there's a question about your smarts."

"I can learn."

"In four hours? The rodeo starts at two o'clock."

A steady stream of pleading on my part before we reached the rodeo arena finally convinced ol' Pickett to give me a lesson in bulldogging. He probably agreed just to get me out of his face. Taking a bunch of pictures of bronc riders and rodeo stock for the *Sun-Leader* was over and done for the moment; instead, fame as a bulldogger performing for Teddy Roosevelt took up residence in my noggin.

Pickett got his horse, Spradley, and a trained hazing pony for me out of the corral. We saddled up and rode over to the holding pens where he talked Charlie Mason into loaning us one of his steers. I found out right away that keeping a steer running straight so a bulldogger could jump on him from a horse required a smart hazer. That was my job to start with. Bill demonstrated how to dive headlong onto the steer, grab his horns and twist his nose skyward. It took enormous strength to plant your heels into the dirt, haul back on the steer's head and bite his snout. After a half dozen go-rounds with Pickett doing it all except biting the steer's lips, he told me to get on ol' Spradley. We were down to the fish or cut bait stage.

By the time I got to jump on that steer, he'd learned more than I had. He avoided my lunge on the first try, causing me to plow a furrow in arena dirt with my chin. He was very adept in dodging the grasp of a leaping smart aleck bent on cranking his neck into a knot. I sort of got the hang of it on my third attempt. Pickett, astride the hazing pony, kept the steer in a straight line while ol' Spradley moved me in close to the critter's left side. I leaned way over, lunged forward, reached over its neck and grabbed the snout.   My other hand grasped the left horn and the heels of my boots dug into the ground as I began to twist his neck. Everything seemed to be going just right until his snout found my face. My teeth went for his lip like an attack dog going for a bowl of table scraps. Instead of lips, I got a mouthful of steer tongue and saliva. I let go, met my shadow on the ground, leaped up and sent spurs to jingling toward the stock tank next to the corral. The gagging and retching ended after I'd gargled and spit out a bunch of tank water. The memory of that experience is bad enough, but Pickett's loud guffawing at such antics was worse. I strapped on my camera and headed for the arena press box.

* * *

By 1:00 p.m., all but the section of seats reserved for Roosevelt and his guests were occupied. The honor of being a photographer for *The Cheyenne Sun-Leader* caused me to flaunt my picture-taking abilities to the four other reporters in the press section.   That ended when free-lance photographer Ralph Doubleday stepped into the box. He was carrying a big, 5 X 7 plate Graflex portrait camera that was manufactured the same year he and I were born. After we said howdy and got acquainted, he showed me all of the features of his Graflex. Old covet crept up on me once more. How I longed to get my hands on that machine. It had a 500-speed roller-blind shutter, but he had added rubber bands to increase tension. With that modification, he was able to freeze the action of a bucking bronc—even a cowboy spread-eagled in midair and headed for a fanny-knocker.

"That sure is some camera," I said, hoping he'd let me get a feel of her.

He didn't catch on to my flattery; instead, he eyed my box camera. "Those are okay for stills, but the shutter speed is a bit slow for action shots."

"Oh! Ezra didn't tell me that."

"Ezra Pheipher?"

"Yep. Y'know Ezra?"

He did. They had been in business together for a time, making and selling picture postcards, before Ezra returned to newspaper reporting. When Ralph explained how successful he had been with that venture, a new inspiration got a hold of me. If I had one of those fancy Graflex cameras, making postcards could bring me fame and fortune. It was something to think about.

Luck smiled on me when the rodeo action was about to begin. Ralph invited me to go with him down to the arena grounds so we could be close enough to get good pictures. We were standing in front of the section reserved for the President when Roosevelt and his guests walked down the isle. As he stepped into the front row, which was draped with red, white, and blue bunting, I had him in my viewer. Before Ralph could thumb his shutter, my camera recorded the moment. That picture made me the first professional rodeo photographer. It was a pity Ralph had to be second, but my future needed all the help it could get. Tom Geiger's first picture postcard had just been exposed.

Just about then, the band began to play the national anthem. A view of the President with hat held over his heart became another latent image on my roll of film. Inspiration really took over my shutter finger. There was a lot of film in my camera and I was determined to expose all one hundred views. I couldn't figure out why Ralph was just standing around with an idle camera in his hand. The answer came swift as a bucking bronc bounding out of a chute. When the rodeo began, he moved around that arena with the agility of a soccer player. He snapped pictures of horses bucking, steers' heads and heels being roped and cowboys getting catapulted into the air. More than once, I almost got myself clobbered by flying hoofs in trying to keep up with him.

When the rodeo ended, I was convinced that nearly a hundred latent images in my camera would bring fame my way. After all, I had gotten most all of the views Ralph had taken.

Ezra failed to tell Mister Collins, the *Sun-Leader* editor, that I would be using a box camera instead of a plate-loaded camera. Since the Kodak folks in Denver had to develop the film and make prints, there would be no pictures available for a week. Collins was madder than a hog sniffing an empty trough. It looked like Ezra and I were both going to be sleeping on a cast-iron bench at the railroad station. Ralph Doubleday saved our fannies when he dropped by the newspaper office before leaving town. He wanted to use Ezra's darkroom to develop his plates. Of course, Collins, agreed—provided he could publish several prints in the next day's edition.

My reprieve was a short one—about seven days. That is when my pictures arrived from Denver. I ripped open the package and dumped the negatives and prints out onto Ezra's desk. All of the action views were distorted and fuzzy. Only six prints were any good: three were of the President at the railroad station; one of him shaking hands with me; one of Roosevelt standing in the bunting-draped section; and one of Teddy standing at attention while the band played the national anthem.

Mister Collins requested my presence in his office after looking at my pile of botched-up pictures. It didn't require a lot of pondering for me to realize what was about to transpire. He asked me to have a seat, and offered me a cigar, which I accepted. At that moment, I wasn't sure I'd get anything else of value for my work. We lit up our stogies and took several puffs while staring at one another. He leaned back in his swivel chair and scratched his baldpate. That's when it dawned on me that he was having a difficult time saying what was on his mind. I didn't feel too sorry for him, because I was the one getting axed. I blew a ring of smoke toward the ceiling, leaned back in my chair and assumed an attitude of comfort by crossing my legs. "What's going to be my next assignment?" I asked, trying to sound like a seasoned photographer.

Now that comment jarred ol' Collins. He nearly swallowed that cigar before he yanked it out of his mouth. "What?" he bellowed. "Assignment?"

It was obvious that my question had hit right in the middle of a sore spot. "The regular Frontier Days Rodeo is coming up in about six weeks," I said, trying to sound confident. "I can get some super pictures with a 5X7 plate, Graflex portrait camera. Y'know, one just like Ralph Doubleday's."

Ol' Collins sat there with his mouth gaping like a calf searching for his mamma's udder. I figured the time was right for me to keep acting like he'd called me in to discuss more assignments. It ain't every day that a boss will offer you a ten-cent cigar unless you were going to get bragged on. That's when I pulled out my six good photographs and spread them on the desk. "Which one do you want to use on my story about the President's visit to Cheyenne?"

Now, if ol' Collins was having a hard time giving me the boot when he called me in, it was getting stickier for him by the minute. He rose up from his chair, leaned over the desk and appeared to ponder my photos. He was close enough for me to get a snoot full of the Bay Rum he had splattered on his face that morning. "How about this one?" I said, picking up the photo of Roosevelt shaking hands with me at the Union Pacific depot.

When he wagged his head, I laid the picture down and selected the one with Teddy standing at attention with hat properly held over his heart. He took the photo, sat down, and chewed on his cigar while scrutinizing the picture. "Well, Geiger," he said, looking me square in the eye. "Sit down here at my desk and write a 300 word article for me."

I had no idea how to use his new Underwood No. 1 typewriter, so a pencil and paper had to do. It took me nearly an hour to write what I wanted to say. It required a while more to get the picture's caption just right. Finally, I was satisfied with the result. Ol' Collins told me to get my fanny out of his chair so he could sit down and read my literary creation.

The caption must have tweaked his funny bone. He glanced at me and began to chuckle. The chuckling kept on while he perused my creation to the end. "Damn, Geiger, I like it, especially your caption. Where did you come up with *Bulldogger Bill Pickett and Friend?*"

I picked up the photo and pointed at the short cowboy standing next to the President. "That's Bill Pickett."

His chuckling turned into belly-bouncing laughter. He slapped me on the back a couple times before he could settle down. "Yeah, I know. Bill Pickett and friend! You're a crafty rascal."

A flood of emotion washed over my soul at that instant. *If ol' Collins were twenty years younger—and a woman --, I'd give him a big kiss.* "Thank you, sir." I said, and then pondered whether to push my luck. *Oh, what the heck.* "When can we order my new Graflex?"

Who Shot Count Rudolph Jäger?

Who shot Count Rudolph Jäger? That was the question being asked by Wyoming cattle barons, newspaper reporters, rustlers and the sheriff of Sheridan County.

I packed some duds, several pencils, a notebook and my new Graflex camera into a valise that my boss, Ezra Pheipher, had loaned me. I was especially proud of all the travel stickers stuck all over its scruffy exterior. Fellow travelers would surmise that its owner was educated in the ways of the world—not a bad guise for a green newspaper reporter/photographer.

I boarded the train at the Cheyenne Depot and headed for my new *Cheyenne Sun-Leader* assignment up at Sheridan, Wyoming. The cattle war in Johnson County had ended in 1892, but events sort of like aftershocks following an earthquake continued to shake the peace and quiet of Wyoming. Count Rudolph Jäger von Rheinfelden, founder and owner of the Lazy J Ranch northwest of Sheridan, had been found dead, lying beside a line shack, the victim of a single gunshot wound in the head. Ol' Rudolph had been a member of the elite barony class of pioneer cattlemen who ruled a major portion of Wyoming's grazing lands. It was rumored that most of the money required to hire Texas gunmen for the cattlemen's invasion of Johnson County in April of 1892 had come from him. Consequently, some figured he'd been waylaid and killed by a gunman hired to mete retribution against the cattle barons. Feelings were running hot after Tom Horn, allegedly employed by the Cattlemen's Association, had been arrested by Laramie County Sheriff Joe Lefors and charged with the murder of young Willie Nickell.

In 1879, Count Rudolph Jäger, member of a German royal family, sold his wine-importing business in New York and headed west. I reckon the wine business wasn't all that exciting—sort of like digging graves and driving a funeral coach. Well, he never looked back after arriving in Wyoming where he established the Lazy J Ranch in the valley along the Tongue River. It encompassed over 75,000 acres of prime grazing land with plenty of water available for his vast ranching enterprise. His death called for an answer. Had Rudolph Jäger committed suicide, been murdered, or was his demise an accident? I intended to find the answer.

Maybe my slapping leather wasn't good enough for becoming a U. S. marshal, but I figured my smarts were up to being an investigative reporter. A burning desire to prove Marshal Tigman's narrow-minded opinion of my talents to be wrong was rekindled as the locomotive chugged into Sheridan.

Lugging Ezra's well-traveled valise, I stepped down from the passenger car and ambled across the street toward the Cowboy Saloon. Ezra said that saloons were always a good spot to pick up information spouted by booze-loosened tongues. All the encouragement needed was to prime the thirst of an unwary subject with a couple of free shots of booze. Then sit back and listen as you ply the poor soul with questions and more whiskey.

The Cowboy Saloon was filled with sounds of intemperate behavior as I shoved my way through the swinging doors. My nose was assaulted by the odors of spilt whiskey, cigar smoke and unwashed cowboys. I set my spurs to jingling toward the bar and sidled myself next to a cowboy attired in a sweat-stained hat, leather vest and chaps. I dropped Ezra's valise, hoping my intended subject would take notice of its travel stickers. "Howdy," I said, trying to sound friendly.

He glanced at the valise. "Howdy."

I pulled out two bits, slapped it on the bar and nodded at the barkeep. "A shot of Jack Daniel's and bring another for my friend."

The barkeep set two shot glasses in front of me, filled them to the brim and picked up my quarter. "That'll be another two bits," he said, holding out his hand.

I fished a silver dollar out of my pocket and flipped it to him. "Leave the bottle."

That's when my intended subject licked his lips and glanced at the nearly full bottle of Jack Daniel's. I had his undivided attention. "Here's to riding a gaited horse, sleepin' beneath a rain tight roof and eatin' high on the hog ever' day of the year," I said, lifting up my glass of Tennessee sour mash whiskey.

"Well, now pard," he drawled reaching for his drink. "I'll sure enough drink t'that."

It took several more toasts and refills before my intended subject said another word. I began to question whether ol' Ezra's tactics were going to work. Finally, my scheme bored in for the kill. "Y'work nearby?" I asked, refilling his glass.

"Yup. The Lazy J."

I felt like the miner who had just slammed a pick into the mother lode. "Y'don't say. How long y'been with the Lazy J?"

"Bout two year."

"Well, that's quite a spell. How's ol' Jäger doin'?"

"He's dead."

I knew the best approach was to act ignorant. "Oh. When did he depart for the big ranch in the sky?"

"Couple months ago."

"How'd he die?"

"Head shot."

"Shot? Who kilt 'im?"

I reckon my question got ahead of the booze. He slammed his glass on the bar and stared at my shocked countenance. "Who's askin'?"

I held up my hands like a defenseless bloke getting ready to receive a right cross to the jaw. "Didn't mean t'pry—just travelin' through."

"Oh, yeah? How'd you come by his name?"

Well, now, that question set me back on my spurs. A quick response had to be forthcoming. Then I remembered a copy of *The Denver Post* that a fellow traveler had abandoned on a bench in the Cheyenne Depot. I unbuckled my valise and pulled out the paper. "See that," I said, pointing at an article on the second page.

He knuckled his bewhiskered chin and peered at the column headline. ***Document Accuses Wyoming Cattle Barons.*** *A penciled letter addressed to recently deceased Cheyenne attorney, Jason Carter, was discovered in his personal files. Carter, a prominent criminal lawyer, had inserted the letter in a brief he was apparently preparing at the time of his death. The letter simply stated the following: Tom Horn, convicted and hanged for the murder of Willie Nickell, was paid over $10,000 by a group of Wyoming cattlemen between 1894 and 1902. Most of the funds contributed were drawn from a Sheridan, Wyoming bank account managed by Humble, Humble and Pierce, attorneys for Count Rudolph Jäger's Lazy J and other Wyoming ranches.*

Hugh Drummond, known to be a Pinkerton detective working out of Denver, signed this letter accusing Wyoming ranchers of contributing funds to a convicted assassin. The Wyoming attorney general's office refused to comment when asked whether an investigation was being considered.

"Well, pard, I still want t'know who's askin'," he said, reaching for the whiskey bottle.

Candor seemed to be called for at this point, so I slapped him on the shoulder and offered my hand. "The name's Tom Geiger."

He had a curious glint in his eyes while sizing me up from my boots to the black stockman's Stetson squared over my eyes. "I'm Jim Fulton," he said, pumping my hand. "What y'doing in Sheridan?"

"Lookin' for work."

"Work?"

"Yup. Is the Lazy J hirin'?"

"Doin' what?

"Well… cowboyin'."

He began to chuckle. "With them hands. They're soft as a baby's butt."

His comment caused me to examine my palms like what he said wasn't so. It was no never mind because he was right. You don't get calluses taking photographs and writing newspaper articles, except maybe on your behind. "I can learn," I said and picked up my whiskey glass.

"Y'got a hoss?"

"Reckon I'll have t'buy one."

"Just what is it that you do—you one o' them Pinkerton fellas?"

It was obvious Jim Fulton didn't buy my being a cowboy looking for work. So, I decided to level with him. "I'm a reporter and photographer for *The Cheyenne Sun-Leader*. My assignment is to determine how Rudolph Jäger met his end."

Ol' Jim began to guffaw something fierce. In fact, he got so loud that everybody in the saloon took notice of his antics. "Aw, come on," I said, refilling his glass. "It ain't that all-fired funny."

His composure was slow in coming. Actually, I had time to down a couple shots of Jack Daniels before his hard-faced demeanor returned an element of sobriety to the situation. It was obvious that my claim needed a bit of proof. "Want t'see my new Graflex?" I said, rummaging through Ezra's valise.

His right hand hovered close to the walnut grip of a Colt .45 slung low on his hip as I rose up with the Graflex in hand. His reaction reminded me of the time Ezra Pheipher took a picture of my disheveled composure on that cast iron bench at the Union Pacific Depot. I was right glad a Graflex didn't resemble a hogleg like Ezra's detective camera. Jim would have ventilated my lean torso with his .45. "Ain't she a beaut'?" I bragged.

"What is that contraption?"

"My camera—want me to take your picture?"

Well, he didn't. By the time the bottle of whiskey was finished, we were nurturing a budding friendship. We staggered over to the Sheridan Inn, paid for a night's lodging and managed to find our rooms on the second floor.

*　*　*

By noon the following day, Jim and I rode into the ravine where Count Rudolph Jäger had been found lying dead beside an isolated Lazy J line shack. The shack was located among aspen and cottonwoods that provided a bit of protection from prevailing Wyoming winds. Jim said it hadn't been used for a couple of years because Jäger bought the Sailing T, a 25,000-acre spread bordering the Lazy J. Consequently, the old property line didn't require a rider anymore. Jim and I stepped out of our stirrups and tied the reins of our hosses, mine rented from the Sheridan Livery, to the shack's hitching rail.

I untied my valise from behind the saddle cantle, unbuckled it and got out my Graflex. While taking pictures of the shack and the exact place where Jim said the Count was found, I plied his recollections. When discovered by him, Jäger's head was lying in a pool of dried blood. There was a single bullet wound behind his right ear. His wallet containing over $500.00 was in his hip pocket. In his right hand was a Colt .45 that had been fired only once. The gun was probably his since the left-handed holster on his left hip was empty. I found it unlikely for him to have shot himself behind the right ear since he was left-handed. Robbery or suicide didn't appear to be valid options.

"What did the sheriff decide happened?" I asked, putting the Graflex back in Ezra's valise.

Jim chunked the ground with the toe of his boot several times while pondering the question. His hesitancy was a bit peculiar since it was such a straightforward inquiry. "Well, he never said."

"Did ol' Jäger have any enemies?"

"More enemies than friends."

"He ever say somebody was out t'get him?"

"Nope."

"You ever hear any threats?"

"Reckon so—'bout half of Sheridan County."

"Who do you think shot him?"

Jim's eyes took on a distant stare. He pulled a sack of Bull Durham out of his pocket and rolled himself a smoke. He struck a match to life across his chaps and lit up. "Nellie done it," he said, blowing smoke around the cigarette dangling from his lips.

"Nellie! Who's Nellie?"

"His missus."

"Jäger's wife?"

"Well, not a real wife. Y'know what I mean?"

Yeah, I knew what he meant. "Cohabiter?"

"A co… what?"

"Livin' together without being married."

"Oh, well sir, I reckon that's what they did. Nellie Tibbits had a hog ranch in Sheridan afore the Count talked her in t'moving in with him."

"Why would she want t'kill ol' Rudolph?"

"Hell," Jim said, rolling his eyes like that was the most stupid question he'd ever been asked. "Look at all this land." He turned around pointing in every direction. "There's a hundred thousand acres in the Lazy J today with over 10,000 head o' white face ranging between the Tongue River and Cloud Peak. Now it all belongs to Nellie."

"How's that? They weren't married."

"The Count ain't got no kids or any relations. He willed it all to her."

It sure looked like Nellie was behind the killing. My main question was whether the sheriff was of that opinion. "Don't y'reckon the sheriff is suspicious of Nellie and her getting all of the Count's earthly possessions?"

"Hah! He's sweet on Nellie. Been hangin' around the Lazy J ever since she moved in."

That is when I began to put everything together. Sure— Nellie and the sheriff were into the killing clear up to their eyebrows. She didn't need to pull the trigger when she had the sheriff panting for her like a dog chasing rabbits. My pictures and story were going to turn Wyoming on its ear. All I needed was to get some photographs of the Lazy J compound, Nellie Tibbits and Sheriff Ben Coburn. Once the story broke, Nellie and Ben would get their comeuppance and I would be on my way to fame and fortune.

* * *

I managed to talk Jim into letting me ride on with him to the Lazy J compound. There was an extra bunk in his bunkhouse where I could stay for a couple of days while winding up my investigation and picture taking.

I'll say this for ol' Jäger; he had built himself quite a spread. The ranch house roof rose almost to the height of surrounding lodgepole pines. It was three stories with seven dormer windows on the third level. There were two barns, several pole sheds, tack sheds, bunkhouses and holding corrals. It was easy to believe why Nellie might covet such an extravagant layout. And ol' Sheriff Ben Coburn was set not only to get Nellie Tibbits in the deal, but he was heading for co-ownership of one of the biggest spreads in Wyoming.

When I saw Nellie the next morning during breakfast, she didn't appear to be mourning much. Of course, if I was right, she had a lot for which to be celebrating. She was a striking figure of a gal—you know—all her parts in the right places. The Count and sheriff couldn't be blamed much for falling for her. She even stimulated my latent urges to sweet talk her into giving up the Lazy J and go traipsing off with a soon-to-be famous reporter and photographer. But, I resisted because I had a job to complete.

I met her while Jim and I were filling our tin plates from platters of beans and bacon on the grub wagon's tailgate. One of the hands passed by leading a sleek bay toward the main house. Nellie, dressed in an English riding habit and boots, came out of the door, crossed the porch, stepped into the stirrup and swung her leg across the saddle. She reined the bay around and cantered toward us. "'Mornin', ma'am," Jim said, tipping his hat.

She reined back the bay and smiled. My insides nearly turned to mush. She was the purtiest gal I'd seen since Doc Ruby ran off with his dancing gal, Fatima. "Howdy, ma'am," I said, smiled and touched the brim of my hat. "Nice mornin' for a ride."

"Yes, it is. Why don't you introduce me to your friend, Jim."

"Yes, ma'am, this here's Tom Geiger."

"Hello, Tom," she said, leaning down to shake my hand. "I'm Nellie Tibbits."

My ol' heart began to palpitate something fierce. "Mighty proud t'meet you, Miz… er… ah… Nellie."

She laughed. I was struck dumb—couldn't say another word. My mouth had turned dry as desert sand; then Jim saved the day for me. "Tom's a newspaper photographer—reckon he's here t'take pictures of you and some of the Lazy J."

Nellie's smile faded. "Which newspsper?"

"Ah, the *Cheyenne Sun-Leader*, ma'am."

"Why do you want pictures of me and the ranch?"

"I'm doin' an article about the purtiest rancher in Wyoming," I said, hoping a little sweet talk might work in my favor.

My lying and being a tad devious worked. She agreed to pose for a number of photographs. They were taken of her astride the bay, sitting atop the corral fence, and standing in front of Count Rudolph Jäger von Rheinfelden's portrait hanging in the sunroom. The session made my spirits soar; however, the experience caused me to ponder the entire venture. Doubt crept into my mind like a coyote stalking a newborn lamb. What was I doing? Could I cause the downfall of such a vivacious and purty lady? I was in a somber mood at the end of the day, having embarked upon self-hatred and remorse.

I was taking pictures of the Lazy J ranch house the following morning when a stranger astride a black gelding rode up to the hitching rail. He was a big fella who sat his hoss straight as ol' Buffalo Bill. He wore a tin star on his leather vest, a holstered Colt .45 tied down to his right thigh, and carried a Winchester rifle in his saddle scabbard. I figured him to be Nellie's admiring sheriff of Sheridan County. "Howdy, Sheriff," I said as he stepped out of his stirrup.

He gave me a once over, probably wondering who was taking photographs of his future home. "Howdy—do I know you?"

"Nope. I'm Tom Geiger."

He glanced at my Graflex. "What are you up to, Tom?"

"I'm doin' a story on the Lazy J for the *Cheyenne Sun-Leader*."

He pondered my performance for a moment while I slid in a new photographic plate. "What makes this ranch so important?"

"Nellie Tibbits… and the Count's death."

"The Count's death comes under my jurisdiction. I'd advise you to leave the investigation to me. Do I make myself clear?"

"Yes, sir. Mind if I take your picture?"

His mood changed from severe to arrogance as he adjusted his vest and squared his Stetson. "Why not. Just remember who's in charge here."

My assurances of full cooperation while shooting several views of him standing next to the gelding seemed to satisfy his humongous ego. I retreated to the bunkhouse when Nellie invited Coburn into the house where he remained most of the morning before riding back to Sheridan. What had they been up to all that time? I had several answers, most of which were conjured up by a jealous mind. But all my imaginings were pure fancy. What I needed were facts. The sheriff's actions were those of a pompous lawman, but he seemed to be straightforward. I couldn't blame him for being sweet on Nellie, which wasn't a crime—unless—they had plotted the Count's demise. I was still determined to find the answers. That's when I decided to ride alone back to the line shack to see what clues might still be there.

* * *

I found the shack to be well stocked with canned food, mostly beans. Its furnishings were: two bunk beds, four ladder-back chairs, an oilcloth-covered table, and a cooking stove. Tinplates, cups, and canisters of sugar, coffee, flour, salt and lard were on a cabinet shelf. A cast iron skillet and a blackened coffeepot were sitting on the stove. An ample supply of cutlery and tableware was stashed in a cabinet drawer. The wood box was filled with split alder logs and tinder for the stove and fireplace. A coal oil lantern hung from a peg in the wall beside the table. All of this was hardly needed if the shack had been abandoned for two years like Jim had said.

I walked through the stand of aspen and cottonwoods surrounding the shack, searching for anything that might be unusual, out of place or suspicious. Finding nothing, I walked back and was about to open the door when I noticed my hoss was gone. He couldn't have gotten away without somebody untying him. I was pondering how that could have happened without me hearing something when a bullet slammed into the shack, barely missing my head. I don't even remember hearing the rifle's report or my opening the door. The next thing I recall was a frantic search inside the shack for a weapon. Somebody intended to end my snooping venture by ventilating my carcass with lead.

The only thing I could find was a nearly hidden double-barrel scattergun in a corner beside the cabinet. Fortunately, I found it to be loaded with two shells of buckshot, but the hammers and mechanism were so rusted I doubted it would even fire. I tossed my hat on the bunk and eased over toward a window, hoping to spot the lowlife back-shooter. I couldn't see anything moving about, only the aspen and cottonwoods swaying in the wind. Suddenly, the window I was peering through shattered as a bullet blew it to smithereens. I thought I was going to be kilt for certain.

I dropped to the floor, clutching the scattergun. My idea about becoming a famous investigative reporter soured as I sat there wondering when the Count's murderer would bust through the door and shoot me dead. I was uncertain about my weapon, wondering whether the triggers and shells might fail due to rust and corrosion. It looked like my grave digging past was about to come home to roost. My only hope seemed to be a run for it after dark, provided the assassin would delay that long. I slid my butt back into a corner behind one of the bunks and waited for the door to fly open. I intended to blast him provided my sorry weapon worked, but that held little consolation.

I sat there listening to my harsh breathing while scrutinizing the shack's four windows and door. My fear continued to mount as sounds around the shack seemed to become more pronounced. Rattling windowpanes, scuffing noises on the roof and high-pitched wailing sounds began to heighten my anxiety. Loose-fitting windowpanes, crumbled chinking between wall logs, and low overhanging tree limbs were being lambasted by the wind. The discordant symphony of sounds never abated until nightfall when the winds died and night critters began their nocturnal chorus. That's when I left my refuge behind the bunk and eased open the door.

With the rusty scattergun ready, my boots carried me out and away from the shack where I took refuge in a thicket of willows growing beside the trail. There I waited for the moon to rise. Only then would there be enough light for me to find my way out of the ravine and head for the Lazy J compound.

About the time the moon rimmed the eastern horizon, I spotted a shadowy figure slinking toward the shack. I didn't trust my weapon, so a decision had to be made—stay in the thicket, head for the Lazy J compound, or sneak up on that rascal and crack his noggin with my not-so-trusty scattergun. Coming out on the short side of most everything in my past became the deciding factor. With a great deal of trepidation, I began to stalk the sneaky backshooter who had crouched down about ten feet from the shack. He probably wasn't sure whether his last bullet had kilt me or not. That suited me just fine, because it gave me a chance to get close enough to wallop a new crease in his Stetson.

It was a rare time indeed, whenever one of my plans had worked. I was bent on success; no more goof ups. As soon as I got close enough to make a swing at him, I stopped. He was squatted still as a frog sitting on a lily pad. The first swat had to connect or I was dead. So, I took aim, swung away, and he fell over like a poleaxed steer. I yanked off my kerchief and tied his hands behind his back—didn't want him to wake up and take offense at what I'd done. Then I rolled him over to see who had tried to do me in. "Jim! Jim!" I yelled. It was Jim Fulton. His eyes were rolled up in his head and he was gasping for air. I figured he'd been kilt for certain. However, pretty soon he began to come around. "Damn Tom, what did y'cold cock me for?"

"Why did y'try to backshoot me?"

He began to pull on his fettered wrists. "Damnit—untie my hands."

"Cain't do that till you tell me why you tried t'kill me."

"What y'talkin' about?"

"Y'stole my hoss and shot at me twice. That's what."

"Now, just one damn minute. I came lookin' for ya when y'didn't get back afore dark."

"Well, if it wasn't you, who could have it been?"

"Don't rightly know, but it wasn't me."

He seemed dead serious and sounded convincing, so I untied his wrists. My big mistake was not lifting his hogleg. That's when I looked down the muzzle of one of Colt's Peacemakers. I'll guarantee you the experience didn't give me any peace. "Okay, Tom," he said, waving his six-shooter toward the shack. "Get your butt inside."

The first thing he did was to tie my wrists with the same kerchief I'd used on him. He lit the lantern, ordered me to recline my carcass on the bunk, and then tied my ankles to the bedstead. I couldn't figure why he just didn't kill me then and there. That's what he'd tried to do all afternoon. It wasn't long before the answer came.

After a couple of raps on the door, Jim opened it. "Come on in. He's tied up on the bunk."

Nellie Tibbits walked in sporting a holstered Colt .45 strapped to her belt. "Did you ask him?" she said, pulling off her riding gloves.

"Nope," Jim said, rubbing the purple lump left by the scattergun. "Figured it best t'wait on you."

She walked over to the bunk, leaned over and patted my cheek. "We don't want to kill you, Tom. We just want to ask a favor."

"Oh! I find that hard t'believe. Ol' Jim did his best t'kill me with two bullets that barely missed my noggin."

"Aw," Jim drawled, "I could've kilt ya easy—just wanted t'scare ya."

"We'll make you a deal, Tom," Nellie said. "When you write your story, just say that Sheriff Coburn killed Rudolph Jäger."

"What reason could the sheriff have for murdering the Count?"

"Jealousy! I turned him down when he asked me to leave Mister Jäger and marry him."

I wasn't anxious to have my bones moldering in Lazy J soil, so playing along was my only hope of getting out of there alive. "Okay—untie me and I'll write the article."

Jim shoved the cold steel muzzle of his hogleg against my neck. "Y'make one move I don't like and you're a dead reporter—y'understand?"

"Reckon I do, untie me."

They did. I pulled my notebook and pencil out of my jacket and sat down at the table. "Tell me how it all came about. I'll write in the sheriff's name like he was the one talking."

Nellie pulled up a chair and sat down beside me. Her closeness got my heart to palpitating all over again. "Just to make sure you don't renege," she said, real breathy like a hog-ranch soiled dove, "I'm going to make you a deal you can't refuse."

"A deal?"

She pinched and then patted my cheek. "The sweetest deal you'd ever hope to get. You do this for me and all 25,000 acres of the Sailing T are yours. I'll even throw in 500 head of prime beef stock." She then pulled a document out of her jacket and laid it on the table. "This is the deed already signed and made out to you. You agree and it's yours."

I didn't have two good choices at that point. If I didn't agree, one more murder at the line shack would take place. If I went along with their scheme, my guilt would be equal to theirs. But, what was I to do?"

I nodded and began to write. The article was to contain an alleged confession made by Sheriff Ben Coburn during a drinking spree at the Lazy J. Jim dictated the conjured up story as to how Count Rudolph Jäger died. The Count and Sheriff Ben Coburn rode up the valley on a Sunday morning to arrest two rustlers who had stocked and been using the remote line shack for their headquarters while raiding Lazy J and Sailing T herds. Coburn had set it up to get Jäger away from the compound to an isolated place where he could be killed. When they reached the line shack, Coburn pulled out his hogleg and shot the Count in the head. Coburn then fired one round out of Jäger's Colt and placed the gun in the Count's right hand, hoping to make it look like a suicide. He then recovered Jäger's spooked hoss and tied him to the hitching rail. When Coburn rode into the Lazy J corral, he told Jim that they failed to get the rustlers. The Count had decided to stay at the line shack for the night, hoping to catch the outlaws if they returned. The following morning, Jim rode up to the line shack where he discovered Count Rudolph Jäger, dead from a bullet wound in the head.

I noticed that Jim couldn't stop pacing the floor all the time he was telling me what to write. He probably had a lot on his mind, the least of which would be what to do about me after finishing the article. Nellie obviously had him in a box. Without any doubt, she had masterminded the entire scenario and wasn't going to share one acre of the Lazy J or Sailing T with anyone— not Jim, Ben Coburn, or me. Once I signed that bogus article, Jim'd kill me. I'm certain she planned to kill him immediately, claiming she tried to save my neck.

"Okay," Nellie said after reading the article. "Go ahead and sign it and you keep the deed."

I felt like I was standing on a gallows, staring at a hemp noose dangling in front of my face. They say the hangman ties thirteen loops above the noose so the victim's neck snaps like a twig when he reaches the end of his rope. I lowered the pencil to the paper, but my hand shook so I couldn't even make a T. I could hear a clicking sound coming from under the table. No doubt, Nellie had just cocked her six-gun. Jim must have heard the click and realized what was in store for him. Well, I'll never know whether she would have kilt ol' Jim or if he would have shot her first. The door flew open and Sheriff Coburn stood silhouetted in the doorway with Colt Peacemakers filling both hands. All hell broke loose as I dived for the floor. When the gunplay was over, Nellie and Jim had lost the battle. Coburn slapped my behind. "I told you I was in charge of this investigation."

Well, I got the real story from Sheriff Coburn. Nellie had agreed to move in with Rudolph Jäger provided he'd will all of his earthly possessions to her in the event of his death. You'd have thought the poor guy would have been smarter than that, but a real looker like Nellie could turn a man's brains into porridge. Then Nellie tried to bait the Sheriff with a tempting proposition. If he would kill the Count, she and the Lazy J plus the Sailing T would be his. He turned her down, but apparently, Jim Fulton had not been able to resist her wiles. The story Jim dictated had been true, only the gunman's name had been changed to protect the guilty.

After I got back to Cheyenne, I finished my article and developed all of the photographic plates. I presented them to Editor Collins, hoping I'd get another cigar and some praises for a job well done. "Let me see your expense account," he said, glancing over my photographs.

I handed him the tally of my expenses and waited. He ran a finger down the list until reaching the final entry. "What's this item? Fifty-five dollars?"

"Now let me think," I said, acting like I'd forgotten what it was for.

"Y'can't remember spending fifty-five bucks?"

"Oh—yeah—now I recall. It was fifteen for a bridle and saddle, and forty for a horse."

"Y'bought a bridle, saddle and a horse? I see up here at the top where you rented a bridle, saddle and horse from the livery."

"Yes, sir, I did."

He sat there chewing on his cigar, waiting for my explanation. "Well..."

"I had t'buy 'em, 'cause they got stolen."

Ol' Collins opened a desk drawer and pulled out a big ledger. He flipped it open and started to pen an entry. "Taking what I owe you from what you owe me leaves you owing fifteen bucks. How do you want to take care of it?"

That's when I pulled out the deed for the Sailing T Nellie had signed and handed it to him. "Reckon I'll have t'owe you until the fall roundup. Is that agreeable?"

Collins looked at me with disbelief raising his bushy eyebrows. "How in the name of Jehovah did you get a ranch deeded to you?"

I leaned over the desk, plucked a Havana stogie out of his humidor and sat down. "Smarts," I said, struck a match and lit my cigar. "What's my next assignment?"

Fabian Fagan's Folly

I met ol' Fabian Fagan in 1910 several years after deciding to quit the newspaper business and take up ranching on the Sailing T, which had been deeded to me by the late Nellie Tibbits. I was sitting on the porch, smoking a Havana cheroot and reading Charles Darwin's *The Descent of Man* when Fagan rode up to the Sailing T ranch house. He was astride a two-humped beast that resembled a camel. However, it was smaller and covered with black and white spots like an appaloosa. To look at Fagan, you would figure him to be a saddle bum who was mooching bed and meals from every ranch in the high country. I had just read about the Neanderthals who had populated part of Europe following the Ice Age. They were supposed to be extinct, but I'd swear the man tying his strange beast to my hitching rail was one of them. He was no more than five and one-half feet in height and wore a weathered "Sugar Loaf' Stetson that emphasized his large head, heavy jaw and receding chin. The prominent brow of his retreating forehead overhung a piercing left eye and a black leather patch shielding his right eye from view. He claimed it had been blinded from a knife allegedly wielded by Bessie Goodnight, a notorious cigar-smoking female gambler. It seems she took offense at his calling her a deck-marking cheat.

For nearly fifty years, he'd been a gambler who had won and lost enough money to buy all of the mineral rights in Alaska. On and on his assertions of adventure unfolded, describing encounters with Arabic potentates and Mongolian tribal chiefs. He had lived with a tribe of Mongols on the high plains east of the Altay Mountains in Outer Mongolia for two years. Camels were highly valued and nurtured by the Mongols, being used to transport heavy loads throughout the high plains and mountains.

During his bragging about his skill in the use of camels, I asked him about the peculiar beast he was riding.

"That fine specimen is a camellama," he replied. "His papa was a llama and his mama was a <u>Camelus bactrianus</u>."

<u>Camelus bactrianus</u> really caught my attention. Here was a throwback human, a spitting image of the Neanderthal man, who was using terms that were beyond my understanding. "What's a <u>Camelus bactrianus</u>?"

"Them are camels with two humps on their backs. They ain't tall as the one-humpers, but they're just as stout and thrive better in high country."

I intended to discover whether he was the biggest fraud or ablest entrepreneur in Wyoming. "Well, now, Mister Fagan, wouldn't you rather have a hoss t'ride?"

"No, sir," he said, biting off a chaw of tobacco. "That critter can out climb, out carry, and outlast any Ass, mule or hoss up here in the mountains. Ridin' him is just like sittin' a rockin' chair."

"Y'don't say. How about workin' cattle?"

Ol' Fagan spat and slapped me on the shoulder. "I've trained him t'do it all. Yes, sir, and he can run fast as the wind besides."

I began to believe Fagan could sell a sheepskin parka to a nomad in the middle of the Sahara Desert. His enthusiasm convinced me that this new crossbreed could work cattle, and also pack heavy loads across the mountains cheaper and faster than mules or oxen. So, I decided to take a closer look at his critter. "Y'mind if I look him over?"

He didn't. In fact, he beat me off of the porch as we headed for the hitching rail. The beast seemed docile enough while I gave him the horse trader's once over. However, he objected when I got to checking his teeth. He grunted and splattered my face with a big glob of spittle. You can't comprehend how gut-wrenching that mishap is if you've never been spit on by a camel or llama.

Fagan ignored all of my antics as I yanked out my kerchief and wiped my face. "Y'want t'ride him? He only spits when y'mess with his lips."

I'd experienced all of the camellama I wanted for one day. I wagged my head and headed for the well to wash my face. All the time, Fagan kept expounding the many virtues and abilities of his alleged crossbreed. While I was pouring a hatful of water over my head, he poked my back with his finger. "Yes, sir, Mister Geiger, a herd of Camellamas would make you a rich man."

Right then I wasn't interested in any animal that had such a vulgar way of telling you to "shove off." However, the more I pondered the idea, the more it made sense. "Y'know where we can get some camels and llamas?"

A grin lifted his scraggly handlebar mustache. "Well, sir, there's a herd o' camels roamin' down in Arizona. We can lasso a couple o' young females and ship 'em up here on the railroad."

"Just females?"

"Yup. We can mate 'em with male Llamas—male camels are too cantankerous and mean."

"We gotta go t'Peru t'get llamas?"

"Aw, naw, we can get them from Ned Bellew's llama ranch down at Pueblo, Colorado."

I figured buying some llamas would be easy enough, but lassoing a camel was sure to be fraught with more problems than catching a roadrunner in a net. Before setting out on such a venture, I had to know a couple of things. "Are you sure camels can thrive up here in the high country?"

"You bet. Like I told ya, camels have been roamin' the mountains of China and Mongolia for a lot o'years."

"You certain o'that?"

He raised his hand like swearing to tell the truth in a court of law. "So help me—that's a fact."

"How'd you come by this camellama?"

"Won him from Zack Miller in a poker game down at Ponca City, Oklahoma."

"Where'd Zack get him?"

"He didn't say—just tol' me it was a rare camellama."

"Y'ever heard of matin' a camel with a llama before?"

"Can't say I have—but my critter is proof that it works. They're both members of the same family. Aint no different from gettin' a mule when y'mate an ass with a hoss."

Well, he did have a point about mules being foaled that way. Right about then, visions of gaining fame and wealth began to nudge my wanta-gets like ol' Satan whispering into the ear of Adam's better half. "Okay—let's go down to Arizona and rope a couple of camels."

*   *   *

Ol' Fabian and I arrived in Tucson, Arizona on the 15th of June. After getting outfitted with two hosses, two pack burros and provisions, we headed for the Mission San Xavier del Bac. Fagan claimed to be a longtime acquaintance of Padre Miguel de Garza who had been the mission priest for more than ten years. Padre Miguel's grandfather had been a pack master under the command of Lieutenant Edward Beale in the early 1860s. Beale had been given command of a camel brigade, which was the brainchild of then Secretary of War Jefferson Davis. Davis proposed that camels would be ideal for hauling supplies from Yuma, Arizona Territory, across the grueling Mojave Desert to Fort Tejon in California. Davis's experiment with camels ended during the Civil War when the brigade was disbanded. The camels were sold, but many were abandoned later to fend for themselves in the arid desert country of southwestern Arizona. Fagan was certain Padre Miguel would be our best source of information regarding the whereabouts of the descendants of those camels.

As we approached the gleaming white-stucco edifice of San Xavier del Bac, a lad of no more than thirteen years came running to meet us. "Señor Fagan, buen día," he said, holding up a canteen.

"Buena mañana, Pablo," Fagan said, leaning down to take the canteen. "Es esta agua fresca?"

"Sí, Señor Fagan. Recepción a la misión."

"Gracias, Pablo. Esta el Padre Miguel aquí?"

"Sí, el Padre Miguel está trabajando en el jardín."

I had no idea what Fagan or Pablo had said. However, I was more surprised that Ol' Fabian could speak Spanish. "What did he say?"

"Well, we just told each other howdy, and he said we will find Padre Miguel in the garden."

After quenching our thirst from the canteen, we followed Pablo toward the garden next to the mission.

Padre Miguel was a small man, no taller than Ol' Fagan; however, he was no Neanderthal. He was pulling weeds from among several rows of melons and potatoes as we tied out hosses next to the garden gate.

"Buen día, Padre Miguel," Fagan called, hurrying to embrace the black-robed priest.

"Buen día. Puedo ver al Señor Fagan."

They stood there speaking Spanish while I waited for Fagan to introduce us. Finally, Padre Miguel stepped toward me with his hand extended. "Soy el Padre Miguel. Ecentado, señor, San Xavier del Bac."

"I'm Tom Geiger," I said, grasping his hand. "Don't reckon I speak Spanish, Padre, but I'm right pleased to make your acquaintance."

"Ah, Señor Geiger, I apologize. I should have spoken to you in English."

After assuring him that there was no offense taken, I got down to the reason for Fagan's and my visit. Yes, his grandfather had been a pack master assigned to Lt. Beale's camel brigade until it was deactivated. All of the camels had been auctioned, most of them being purchased by freighters to haul mail and other cargo from San Pedro to Los Angeles. His grandfather had purchased six of the camels to use in a nefarious exploit of transporting bullion from Virginia City, Nevada to Santa Fe, New Mexico Territory. The gold would then be carried by freight wagons to El Paso where it was to be loaded onto a train bound for Richmond, Virginia and the coffers of Jefferson Davis's Confederacy. Unfortunately, the camel caravan never made it to Santa Fe. His camels later were discovered roaming up and down the Colorado River basin in

Arizona and southern Utah. Padre Miguel's grandfather de Garza and the gold were never heard of again.

While sitting in the Padre's quarters, I was beginning to believe our sojourn would be for naught. Few camels had been seen in southwestern Arizona for several months. The padre could only recall rumors about a herd of less than a dozen being sighted by a prospector in the desert near Gila Bend. I was about to forget about roping camels and breeding them with llama's when Ol' Fagan spoke up. "Padre Miguel, usted se olvidó de los camellos Blanco's."

The Padre glanced at me and wagged his head. "Señor Fagan, we must speak only English. Señor Geiger doen't understand Spanish. Yes, I did forget about Señor Blanco's camels."

"Who's Señor Blanco?" I asked.

"My grandfather knew the man called Blanco very well. They were hired to teach the soldiers how to pack the camels. When the brigade was disbanded, Señor Blanco bought several to start a freighting business between the Colorado River ports and Tucson."

"Yeah," Fagan said, "I remember your grandpa telling how some Apaches killed ol' Blanco and stole all of his camels. Don't know why they wanted 'em. Sure wouldn't try t'eat one."

"Pablo, tráigame por favor mi de segueidad fuerte," Padre Miguel called. "I just asked Pablo to bring my strong box. I have something to show you."

When Pablo returned with the strong box, Padre Miguel produced a brass key from his cassock and opened the lock. He rummaged through the contents until discovering a leather wallet. He hesitated for a moment, seeming to be in deep contemplation. "Ah, si," he said, "esta perteneció al Señor Blanco. This wallet belonged to Señor Blanco. A Chiricahua Apache woman left it hanging on the mission gate many years ago—a long time before I arrived."

Padre Miguel handed the wallet to me. "Inside you will find a map. On the map is an X. This marks Señor Blanco's camp near the Colorado River. That is where the Chiricahua Apache killed Señor Blanco and stole his camels."

The wallet was quite old and weathered. Señor Blanco de Diego was stamped in gold across the front. I retrieved the map, which was yellowed and brittle from age. It was a crude drawing with little semblance of a cartographer's work. I quickly found the X, which was located near the coming together of Colorado and Gila rivers. The mark was smudged with a purplish smear—no doubt, dried blood. I folded the map and placed it back into the wallet. "Why would a woman leave this hanging on the mission gate?" I asked, handing it back to the padre.

"No one ever knew. Most likely, it was done to free the Apache from a curse."

"A curse?"

"Si, they worshipped supernatural beings called ga'ns, protective spirits that governed their lives. Returning the murdered Blanco's wallet to the mission was probably an act dictated by their religion—medicine to drive away evil spirits."

Ol' Fagan slapped his thigh. "That's it!" he yelled, jumped up and whacked my shoulder. "Bet them camels were the devils they wanted to get away from."

"That makes sense," I said. "Reckon they kilt the camels?"

"Bet they turned 'em loose—ran them stinky critters plumb across the border."

Padre Miguel returned the wallet to the strong box and closed the lock. "If they did, you will most likely find them somewhere southwest of here—maybe in Mexico."

* * *

The next morning we rode through the mission gate and headed southwest. I was wishing Ol' Fagan had never set foot on the Sailing T. We were on a wild camel chase if there ever was such a thing. The idea of mating camels and llamas to produce a camellama was fraught with a lot of doubt about whether it was even a possibility. Now I was in the middle of the Sonora Desert with a Neanderthal, riding strange hosses and leading two asses loaded down with provisions. What were we about? Hunting for camels that probably didn't even exist, and if they did, how in Jehovah's name would we ever be able to rope two females and get them back to Tucson. I was feeling lower than a Gila monster's belly, which was a local reptile that might just decide to crawl into my bedroll some night and sharpen his teeth on my carcass. The only thing that kept me going was pride—I'd be laughed clear out of Wyoming if I went home without any camels. Then again, they would probably laugh harder if we unloaded a couple of those critters at the Sheridan depot. And there was the matter of water. We had enough in a keg on one of the asses for a couple of days, so we had to find water somewhere or the buzzards would have a repast.

Ol' Fagan seemed to sense my mood. He sidled next to my hoss and offered me a chaw of tobacco. "It'll ease your thirst."

At the moment I couldn't imagine anything worse than champing my teeth together on a wad of tobacco. "No, thanks—don't use it."

"Buck up. Ol' Blanco's camels are out here. I can dang near smell 'em."

"I tell you what, Señor Fabian Fagan de la Mancha, we're two fools chasin' windmills in the middle of the desert."

"Huh—what y'talkin' about? The heat got ya already?"

"It ain't the heat. I just realized that we are on an idiotic expedition like the guys Miguel de Cervantes wrote about. I'm Don Quixote and you're his squire, Sancho Panza, and we're jousting windmills out here in the Sonora Desert."

I don't reckon Ol' Fagan had any idea what I was talking about. If he could speak Spanish as well as English, I figured he aught to know how to read. "Y'ever read the book, Don Quixote, by Señor Cervantes?"

"Nope, never have. What's he got t'do with ropin' a couple of camels?"

"Never mind. Forget I mentioned it."

For the following two days, we wandered farther to the southwest without sighting anything except saguaro and organ pipe cacti. Early in the morning of the third day, we arrived at Sonora Wells in Mexico. I was drawing water from the village well to replenish the water keg and water our animals when Ol'

Fagan slapped my backside. "Look yonder," he said. "Told ya I could smell camels."

He was right. Silhouetted on the western horizon and heading toward Sonora Wells was a string of camels; all of them, except the leader, carried large packsaddles loaded with cargo. A man wearing a wide-brimmed sombrero was sitting the lead camel. As the caravan approached, it became obvious that these camels had two humps, which proved they were not descendants of the one-humped animals used by the U. S. Army in Arizona and California. I then took notice of the caravan's cargo. "What is that apparatus?" I asked my trusty squire, pointing at the device strapped atop the second camel.

Ol' Fagan gawked at the contraption for a moment. "Well, I'll be damned. That's a disassembled Gatling gun."

"You sure of that?"

"Yep—we used one during our charge up San Juan Hill."

"You fought with Ol' Teddy in Cuba?"

"Shore did."

That was an unexpected revelation about the strange Neanderthal standing beside me. Whether he did or not wasn't important. He seemed to recognize the lethal weapon being transported to who knows where. Then I scrutinized the fellow riding the lead camel. His face was hard to make out in the shade cast by the sombrero, but double braces of cartridge belts strapped across his chest identified him to be an outlaw or soldier. I hoped it was the latter. "What do you make of this?"

"Don't rightly know, but you stay here while I go palaver with that hombre."

I watered the horses and asses while Ol' Fagan walked out to meet the double-braced stranger. Their conversation went on for quite a while. Neither Fagan nor the rider made any gestures during their confrontation—only nodding and wagging of their heads indicated agreements or otherwise. Finally, the rider's camel knelt down on his knees and the stranger dismounted. He and Fagan walked over to the well where I was tending our animals. "This here is Señor Jesús Juárez," Fagan said, nodding at the man wearing a sombrero.

"Mighty proud t'meet ya," I said, accepting his handshake. "I'm Tom Geiger."

"Welcome to Mexico, Señor Geiger," he said. "Señor Fagan says you are hunting for camels."

This fellow, obviously a Mexican, spoke English with very little accent. "Yes, Señor Juárez, we are."

"There are no camels in Mexico except for mine, which are used to transport supplies to the forces of Señor Doroteo Arango, the one you call Pancho Villa."

"No camels except yours?"

"None, Señor Geiger."

"I see. Well, would you consider sellin' a couple of 'em?"

Juárez eyed our hosses, asses and me for a moment, and then smiled. "Si, Señor, I will consider an offer."

"How much y'think they're worth?" I asked Fagan, hoping he had some idea what the going price would be.

He walked over to the waiting caravan and scrutinized each camel. While he was going from beast to beast, Juarez was doing the same to our hosses and asses. It appeared that he was interested in making a swap with an unknown amount of cash to boot. Finally, Fagan returned. "Maybe two-hundred apiece—no more than two-fifty."

I glanced at Juárez . His expression revealed nothing. "Oh, Fagan. They don't look to good t'me," I said, hoping to diminish Juárez's expectations.

"You can have your pick of two of them for six-hundred American dollars, plus your horses and burros."

"That's a mighty stiff price, Señor Juárez. Make it three-hundred, plus our animals."

"Four-hundred, plus them, and two camels are yours."

I glanced at Fagan. He nodded. "Okay, it's a deal."

After paying the agreed price and loading all of our supplies on one of the two camels, Ol' Fagan and I bid adios to Señor Juarez. That is when I got an education about dealing with Mexican revolutionaries. Juárez unholstered his hogleg and motioned for Fagan and me to step away from our camels. "I'm sorry, Señor Geiger, but I have decided not to let you take the camels."

"What y'mean? A deal is a deal?"

"No—this is Mexico. We are at war with Porfirio Diaz. The leader of our revolution, General Madero, has need of your camels."

"Okay—so y'changed your mind. We'll load our stuff on the burros and head back t'Tucson."

"Oh, I am sorry. The horses, burros, and your pistols belong to the General. Please unbuckle your holsters, drop them and step away."

Well, I can say one thing for Señor Juárez. He was a slick highwayman. Instead of trying to kill Fagan and me when he rode into Sonora Wells, he had disarmed us with his charming guise. After handing over my gold pocket watch to him, Juárez then waved his hogleg toward the horses. "Please," he said with a tone of apology in his voice. "I invite you to ride my horses. We have a long way to travel."

Ol' Fagan finally found his tongue. "Just where are we headed?"

"Oh, Señor Fagan, I cannot tell you. You will see."

"How can I express my gratitude, Señor Juárez?" I said, stepping into my stirrup. "I'm overwhelmed by your kindness."

Fagan leaped astride his hoss and reined him around to face me. "Y'better make a list of stuff t'thank him for, 'cause we're in for a lot more treats."

By the time we reached our destination, which happened to be the encampment of Pancho Villa's rebels, I had become accustomed to the ways of two-humped camels. They were even more disgusting than llamas. They not only spit when exhibiting displeasure but seemed to take delight in slobbering all over my head and face. They would also bray low-pitched gurgling sounds that sounded like a boiling Yellowstone mud pot. And, they delighted in nipping my backside with their incisors like a cantankerous hoss. Consequently, I was more than relieved as we rode into the mountain encampment of the rebels.

After turning his caravan over to two well-armed men, Juárez escorted us to a large tent located near the center of the encampment. Loud voices coming from within the tent sounded as if there were significant disagreements being argued. A guard stepped in front of the entrance. "Alto! Quiénes son estos hombres?" he said to Juárez, pointing a large revolver at me.

"Estos hombres son mis presos. Debo hablar con el general."

The guard nodded and stepped aside. He held up his hand, making it quite clear that Fagan and I were not to accompany Juárez. I was beginning to pick up on a few Spanish words, but not enough to know what was said. "What did they say?" I whispered to Fagan.

"The guard wanted to know who we are and ol' Juárez said we were prisoners."

"Who do you reckon is in this tent?"

"The guy who's going to decide whether we see the sun come up tomorrow."

That bit of information wasn't what I wanted to hear. I glanced around the encampment. It was crawling with a lot of men, some young, and some old enough to have white hair and beards. Most of them seemed to ignore our existence, but two hombres squatting next to a campfire were watching us with more than curious interest. The sight was disconcerting. The hackles on the back of my neck began to crawl as I whispered to Ol' Fagan. "How are we going t'get out of this mess?"

Before Fagan could answer, Juárez appeared in the entrance and motioned for us to enter. I'll never forget what happened after we stepped into that tent. There were three men seated around a small table. Each of them wore double braces of cartridge belts strapped across their chests. The man, seated in the middle, smiled and gestured for us to come closer. He appeared to be in his mid-thirties, was clean-shaven with the exception of a large mustache, and had piercing black eyes that quickened my fear to a new level. "Gentlemen," he said in heavily accented English. "My comrade, Señor Juarez, tells me that you have contributed all of your possessions to the revolución. Is this true?"

" Well, Señor… Ah… "

"Villa—Francisco Villa," he said, extending his hand, which I accepted with a lot of enthusiasm.

"I'm Tom Geiger."

"And who is your compañero?" he said, nodding at Fagan.

"He is Señor Fabian Fagan."

"Why, Señor Geiger and Señor Fagan, did you gentlemen come to Mexico?"

"To get a couple of camels."

"Camels?"

"Yes, sir, y'see Señor Fagan and I plan to breed a couple of camels with some llamas."

Señor Villa's eyes grew wide and questioning. "Serious you cannot be, Señor Geiger. Mate a camel with a llama? That is unbelievable."

I poked ol' Fagan in the ribs. "Tell him about your camellama."

My trusty squire cleared his throat a couple of times—no doubt trying to quiet his anxiety. "Well now, General Villa, what Tom says is true. Y'see, I have a camellama, which is an offspring of a two-humped camel and a llama. He is a sturdy animal, smaller than a camel but larger than a llama that can pack nearly as much weight as a camel. He has the good nature of a llama and can thrive in high mountains. We figure to raise a lot of camellamas to transport supplies and gold ore between mountain mines and the railroads."

Villa stared at us for a moment after Fagan stopped talking. Then he turned to speak with the two fellows seated next to him. They did a lot of hand waving and arguing for several minutes before Villa spoke to us. "Where is this camellama?"

"He's on my ranch, the Sailing T, in Wyoming."

"Wyoming?"

"Yeah—y'know—the United States."

"I know where Wyoming is, but your story is, how do you say, an ideado, an invention?"

Ol' Fagan pulled out his wallet, removed a photograph of his camellama and handed it to Villa. "That's my camellama."

The three rebel leaders pored over the picture while discussing Fagan's weird beast. Finally, Villa returned the photo to Fagan. "My comrades and I have made a decision. We are not going to shoot you."

"Well, sir," I said, trying to sound calm. "We appreciate that."

"You are welcome. But you still haven't answered whether you have contributed your possessions to the revolución."

I immediately knew any reply other than that we had done so would be a stupid answer. "Yes, sir, we did."

"Gracias, mis amigos. Now I have another request."

Something whispered in my insides that we were about to be given another choice that would determine whether we would walk out of the rebel's encampment. "You're welcome. What is it we can do for you?"

"Do you know how to operate a Gatling gun?"

"I sure do," Fagan said, "but my compañero doesn't."

Villa smiled. "He looks like a bright hombre—can you teach him—and the rest of my commrades?"

My trusty squire glanced at me and nodded. "Reckon so."

General Villa stood up and offered his hand. "Bueno, mis amigos. Welcome to the revolución. Viva Méjico."

I accepted Pancho Villa's outstretched hand after Fagan elbowed me in the ribs. At first, my enthusiasm failed to rise to the occasion; however, the piercing eyes of Señor Villa conveyed a stimulating message to my reluctance. "Yes, sir," I said, wringing Pancho's hand. "Viva Méjico—long live the revolución."

A wide grin lifted his mustache "Ah, spoken like a true compañero," he said, gripping my hand tighter with each word he spoke. "We will defeat Porfirio Diaz and his soldados. I, you, and Señor Fagan, one day will raise the banner of General Madero over Ciudad de Méjico."

Well now, that brag hit a hollow note in my noggin. I wasn't about to become a soldier in Pancho Villa's rebel army. At least, not long enough to attain victory for the rebels. That might require more years than I had left. But, what were my trusty squire, Fabian Fagan, and I to do? My trepidations were suddenly interrupted when Fagan snapped to attention and saluted our host. Villa returned the salute and stood unmoving with his eyes fixed on my shaking composure. It didn't take long for me to figure what he was waiting for. I snapped my shoulders back, clicked my heels together like a Prussian officer, and flipped my hand above my brow. "Yes, sir, General Villa," I said, standing at attention.

Villa nodded and dropped his hand. "Compañero Juárez will return your pistols. You will need them tomorrow."

I resumed my usual posture of nonchalance. "What's happening tomorrow?"

"We ride at dawn for El Fuerte to rob the train that carries mucho silver ingots."

I glanced at Fagan who shrugged his shoulders. We had gone from wandering across the Sonora Desert in search of camels to being prisoners of Pancho Villa somewhere in the Sierra Madre Mountains of Mexico. Tomorrow, we would become train-robbing outlaws—not a very promising future. I envisioned our being captured by Diaz's soldados and then facing a firing squad in front of a bullet-pocked stone wall. Villa grinned, no doubt amused by the expressions of dread contorting the faces of Fagan and myself. "Do not fear," he said, slapping the six-shooter cradled in a holster on his right hip. "It has all been arranged. You will see."

Villa proceeded to explain that Señor Salinas, the alcalde of El Fuerte was a compadre of General Madero. He had agreed to detain the departure of a train loaded with silver ingots valued at 100,000 pesos bound for the coffers of President Diaz in Mexico City. Señor Salinas had also assured General Madero that there would only be two soldados guarding the ingots. The guards had been converted to the revolution by coercion and bribes. There would be no resistance for taking the silver and diverting it to the cache that was financing their rebellion.   It would buy many Yankee rifles and much ammunition for the first battle planned by Madero and Villa. Time was growing short. Villa bragged that the revolución was to be launched in November, at which time the rebels planned to attack Piedras Negras, in the state of Coahuila.

Fagan and I spent a sleepless night. We were in deep trouble and headed for more. I figured it was sort of like stepping into a bog of quicksand—no matter what we did to resist the events that had taken over our destiny, we were up to our necks in muck. I was certain that we had to get out of there. But—how—that was the question.

At first light, we mounted up for the two-day ride to El Fuerte. Our raiding party consisted of Pancho, six compañeros of the revolución, Fagan and me. The terrain was rugged, but no more so than the high country of Wyoming. Even though Villa had returned our hoglegs, it was obvious that he and his compatriots did not trust us. Each time I tried to ride next to Fagan, one of the rebels reined his hoss between us.

It wasn't until we camped the first evening that I was able to speak with my trusty squire. While we were dining on beans and tortillas, I squatted next to Fagan. We were far enough away from the others that it seemed safe to discuss our predicament. "Y'been to El Fuerte before?" I asked Fagan.

"Yup," he said through a mouthful of beans.

I wasn't surprised by his reply. It seemed that he had been every other place in the world—so why not El Fuerte? "Y'got any ideas how to get out of this mess?"

"Shore do, got a plan all laid out."

"You do?"

"Yup."

"Well, what is it?"

"While ol' Pancho and his compañeros are busy stealing the silver, we ride hell bent for Los Mochis."

His idea sounded good, but I had very little hope that it could happen. "Where is Los Mochis?"

"Southwest of El Fuerte, near the coast."

"Even if we can get to Los Mochis, where do we go from there?"

"Topolobampo, about 15 miles from Los Mochis. We can board the first ship headed for Los Angeles."

Well, I figured if Fagan knew about Los Mochis and Topolobampo, he must know the area. Since I didn't have any plan for an escape, making a run for it when we arrived at El Fuerte had to do. "Okay—Let's do it."

* * *

We rode into El Fuerte after dark. It was a city founded in 1564 by the Spanish conquistador Don Francisco de Ibarra, the first explorer of the western Sierra Madre Mountains. In 1610, a fort was built to ward off the fierce Zuaque and Tehueco Indians. El Fuerte was the gateway to the last frontiers of Sonora, Arizona and California. We tied our hosses to the depot's hitching rail. A locomotive and several boxcars were parked on a siding next the loading dock. Pancho assured us that the silver cache was in the second car behind the locomotive's coal tender. The guards were nowhere to be seen, an oddity in my opinion. We walked through the depot with Pancho leading the way. The waiting area was also empty—another oddity. As we approached the railcar in question, I glanced at Fagan. He wagged his head as if to say, "not now."

Pancho rapped his fist against the car door and demanded it be opened in the name of General Madero. Only silence came from the car. Pancho rapped again. "Abra la puerta!"

Suddenly, there was the sound of many boots running onto the loading dock. I spun around as a squad of soldados fell into formation between the depot and us. They held bayoneted rifles at the ready while their leader, a young sergeant barely old enough to shave, stepped forward. He stood at attention and saluted while speaking to Pancho. I had no idea what he had said, but one by one, Pancho and his compañeros obeyed the soldado's order by laying down their weapons and raising their hands. Again, I glanced at Fagan. He nodded, tossed his hogleg on the dock and raised his hands. With regret, I did the same. There wasn't going to be any riding hell bent for Los Mochis.

About that time, a man stepped from the depot and confronted Pancho. "Buenas noches—Señor?"

Pancho grinned. "Villa, General Pancho Villa. Buenas noches, Señor Salinas. I presume you speak English?"

"Of course, welcome to El Fuerte, General Villa. Why do you ask?"

Pancho nodded at the sergeant. "What I have to say is confidential."

"I understand."

"My compañeros and I are here to get the silver ingots for General Madero."

Señor Salinas frowned and gestured for Pancho to come closer. They stood facing each other and began speaking so low it was impossible to hear what they were saying. After considerable negotiations had gone on, Salinas called for the sergeant to join them. More discussions transpired before Salinas said anything to the rest of us. He walked over to confront Fagan and me. "General Villa says you are North Americans."

"Yes, sir. I'm Tom Geiger and my friend is Fabian Fagan."

"General Villa tells me that you have joined the revolución. Why did you do this?"

Suddenly, I had an inspiration. We had no arms. There was a squad of soldiers ready to stand us up against a wall and end our sojourn into Mexico. It looked like the simple plan Villa claimed to have in place had gone awry. Without consulting my trusty squire, I spoke my piece. "I'd sure like to know who I'm talkin' to."

Salinas nodded as we shook hands. "Of course. I am Señor Alfredo Salinas, the mayor of El Fuerte."

"Mighty proud to meet ya, Señor Alfredo Salinas. Mr. Fagan and I came to Mexico in search of a couple of camels."

"Camels? In Mexico?"

I'll say one thing; Salinas was a good listener. After telling him the whole story, he began to laugh. In fact, his laughter was so contagious that pretty soon the soldados and rebels, including Pancho, were guffawing. It made no never mind to me provided Fagan and I could save our necks and get the heck back to Wyoming.

Sobriety finally returned when Salinas stopped laughing. "Señor Geiger," he said, wiping his eyes with what appeared to be a white silk handkerchief. "Señor Villa and I have reached an agreement. We have decided to divide the silver ingots between us. Half will go to Generals Madero and Villa, one-fourth will go to Señor Villa's compañeros, which includes you and Señor Fagan, and the remainder will remain here with me for safekeeping." He emphasized *safekeeping* with a wink. "That means you and Señor Fagan will get a goodly sum of pesos. Is this fair?"

That agreement got ol' Fagan's attention. "How much will each compañero get?"

"3,125 pesos."

"Yes, sir, that's fair enough. Got any cantinas in El Fuerte?"

"Oh, yes, we have several. I happen to own the finest cantina. It is in the Posada del Lujo, the most luxurious hotel in all of Sinaloa."

I kept eyeing the soldados and their young sergeant. They probably couldn't understand English, but it seemed they could easily veto everything Salinas and Villa had decided. "What about the soldiers?"

Salinas held a finger to his lips and leaned closer. "Do not be concerned. I will take care of them."

I was sure that he would. There were a lot of dividing-the-spoils going on—all interested parties got their share. It was how everyone got along; an ancient system which seemed to work.

The confrontation at the railroad depot ended by the mayor of El Fuerte inviting everyone to spend the night in his hotel—for a reasonable charge, of course.

* * *

My trusty squire and I walked into the Posada del Lujo, the most luxurious hotel I'd ever seen. Salinas claimed it required five years and 100,000 gold pesos to build. Its lavish furnishings were brought by boat from San Francisco, California, unloaded at Topolobampo Bay, and then transported to El Fuerte by oxen-drawn wagons. We didn't stop to register for our rooms. The sounds of gaiety coming from the Posada del Lujo Cantina pulled Fagan and me across the lobby and through a limestone archway. The odors of spilt tequila, cheap perfume and cigar smoke seemed to set the mood for the evening. We'd hoist some booze, smoke Cuban cigars, play a little poker and get acquainted with the ladies of the night. Pancho had promised all of his compañeros, including Fagan and me, that we were to "live it up"—everything was on the revolución. So, that is what we intended to do.

As we stepped up to the bar, Fagan bellowed for a bottle of tequila and some cigars. The bartender glanced at us and frowned. "Un momento, los Señores."

"Don't know what he's scowlin' for—only asked for a bottle of tequila and some cigars."

"You might have gotten faster service if you had said por favor, Señor."

"Yeah, reckon sayin' please don't hurt."

While waiting for our booze, I glanced about the cantina. Through the drifting smoke, I spied three ladies who looked up and smiled from the satin covered sofas where they sat. One señorita was especially pretty—black hair flowing across bare shoulders, and dark eyes that flashed in the orange lamplight. She appeared to be no more than twenty. Once again, she smiled and tucked her head, no doubt trying to feign innocence. I reckon my rapt attention caught Fagan's curiosity. He laughed and nudged me in the ribs. "She's a real looker, ain't she?"

The comment reflected his crude Neanderthal character, but he was right. She was quite a "looker."

The bartender slid two glasses and a bottle of tequila onto the bar and held out his hand. Fagan reached for the bottle. "Por favor, we are compañeros of Señor Villa. Comprende? He will pay."

The bartender nodded and offered us two Cuban cheroots. After lighting up, Fagan filled our glasses with tequila. I looked at the dark-eyed beauty, raised my glass and nodded. Instead of tucking her face this time, she stood up and walked toward me. Fagan leaned closer and whispered. "Well now compadre, looks like y'got a nibble."

"Reckon so," I said. She reminds me of Rosa."

"Who's Rosa?"

"Oh, she and I learned to dance the Flamingo at White's Saloon in Casper a lot of years ago."

Fagan downed his tequila in one swallow. "Well, compadre, reckon I'll just mosey around—find myself a game of poker, or maybe a señorita."

I raised my glass as the young lady approached. "Buenas noches, señorita. May I offer you a drink?"

Her eyes danced as she nodded. "I would love to have a drink with you, Señor...?"

I bowed a tad to show my respect. "I'm sorry. Thomas, er I mean Tom. Tom Geiger."

"I am pleased to meet you, Señor Tom Geiger. My name is Señorita Margarita Salinas."

"Salinas?"

"Si—yes, Señor Alfredo Salinas is my father."

Now that was the surprise of a lifetime. I really didn't know what to say. I supposed that any señorita sitting in a cantina without an escort was a soiled dove—a lady of the night. No respectable father, especially the mayor of El Fuerte, would allow his daughter to be a common trollop in his own cantina. "Let's find a table where we can visit."

"Si, that would be nice," she said, slipping her hand around my elbow. "Come, I will take you to one of my father's private tables in the patio garden."

A covered archway and guest rooms bordered the patio, which was located in the center of the hotel. Several tables were placed around a pool that was covered with water lilies. Candles burning in hurricane lamps on each table filled the patio with flickering lights and dancing shadows. Margarita led me to a table on the edge of the patio where her father and another man were engaged in conversation. As we approached the table, Señor Salinas stood up. "Ah, Señor Geiger, I see you have discovered my lovely daughter." The other man then stood up as Salinas gestured toward him. "I would like to introduce you to my compadre, General Madero."

The General was not an impressive fellow. His attire was rather plain, but his smile captured me. I could see why he was considered to be a leader, one who could inspire men like Pancho Villa and Alfredo Salinas to join him in rebellion against Porfirio Diaz. "Mighty proud t'meet ya, General Madero," I said, reaching for his outstretched hand.

"And I am pleased to welcome you to Mexico, Señor Geiger."

Señor Salinas requested Margarita and me to join them. He waved his hand at a waiter, who then brought wine and glasses to our table. "Let us drink to the revolución," Salinas said, pouring wine into our glasses.

"Si, Señor Salinas," General Madero said, gesturing toward Salinas, Margarita and me. "Viva Mejico. Viva la revolución."

After we imbibed several glasses of wine and made toasts to the revolution, I began to feel a bit giddy. The conversation quickly centered on the coming hostilities between the rebels and the soldados loyal to Diaz. Madero seemed to have complete confidence in my loyalty to the cause. He had just returned from San Antonio, Texas, where he had taken refuge from Diaz and his heavy-handed soldados. While he was in exile, he had written the "Plan of San Luis," which was a manifeto declaring the elections fraudulent; therefore, Porfirio Diaz could not be the legitimate President. Madero proceeded to declare himself President Pro-Temp until new elections could be held. He promised to return all land, which had been confiscated from the peasants. He further demanded that any future president be limited to one term in office. I was beginning to wonder whether this self-proclaimed president and general might be suffering from delusions of grandeur. But I discovered later that sort of behavior wasn't unusual in Mexico's politics. Finally, Madero pulled a map from his pocket and spread it across the table. "Señor Geiger, have you had any military training or experience?"

"No, sir, but my friend, Fabian Fagan, claims to have fought with Colonel Roosevelt in Cuba."

"Perhaps you could persuade Señor Fagan to join us."

"Reckon I can. I'll go fetch 'im."

Margarita and I excused ourselves and went looking for my trusty squire. We found him playing poker with three of the compañeros. He seemed to have been doing well, because a significant number of chips were piled on the table in front of him. I tapped his shoulder and leaned over to whisper in his ear. "Hey, Fagan, Salinas and General Madero would like for you to come to their table out on the patio."

"Right now? Look at this hand," he said, spreading his cards for me to see."

He had a pair of black aces, a pair of black eights, and a queen of spades. "Y'might want to fold right now—you're holdin' Wild Bill Hickok's dead man's hand."

"Y'mean the hand he had when ol' Jack McCall kilt 'im?"

"Yep, that's the hand."

Fagan folded his cards and dropped them on the table. "Reckon I've got t'fold, compañeros," he said stuffing the chips he'd previously won into his pocket. "General Madero wants my advice on somethin'."

I was glad to get away from Salinas and Madero so Margarita and I could spend the evening together. Instead of returning to the patio, we discovered a vacant sofa near the entrance to the cantina. There, we got acquainted, raised several glasses of tequila and toasted ourselves—no more salutes to the revolución. Then the highlight of the evening came when a fellow wearing a black sombrero trimmed with gold designs stopped in front of our sofa. He began to strum a guitar and sing for us. I couldn't understand the Spanish lyrics, but I didn't really care when Margarita began to snuggle closer to me. After singing a couple of songs, he leaned over and held out his hand. He seemed disappointed when I gave his hand a big Wyoming shake. "Por favor," he said. "In Méjico, you pay for music."

I happened to have some Yankee dollars left in my wallet, so I handed him a sawbuck. He snapped the bill taut a couple of times and grinned. "Gratia, Señor. I play more for you."

Well, I'd had enough wine and tequila to embolden myself. "How about something hot—y'know—music for dancing the flamingo."

"Ah, Si, you dance flamingo with Señorita Salinas?"

Margarita apparently wasn't convinced that a Yankee cowpoke from Wyoming could dance the flamingo. She held a handkerchief to her mouth and began to laugh. "I sure can," I said, reaching for her hand.

Our troubadour yanked off his sombreo, tossed it on the floor and yelled. "Las damas y los caballeros--Señorita Salinas y el Señor Gringo bailarán el flamenco.

With sounds of raucous applause filling the cantina, I led Margarita to the sombrero. I assumed the pose of a bullfighter preparing to receive a charge from El Toro. Margarita's eyes flashed as she swung herself into position. There we stood, facing each other, waiting for the music to begin. When our troubadour swept his fingers across the guitar strings, we began to dance. Faster and faster, he played until sweat began to sting my eyes. My spurs hadn't jingled that much in years. Margarita was flawless in her steps and twirls that made her skirt fly higher than Rosa's ever did. It was just like old times in White's Saloon at Casper, Wyoming when Jake Tillie and I did the flamingo with Maggie and Rosa. That moment, I fell in love with Margarita Salinas. Before the music stopped and our heels quit slapping the floor, I made a decision. I wasn't going back to Wyoming without Margarita. If I had to stay in Mexico, join the revolución and get shot at by Diaz's soldados, I would consider doing it.

When the music stopped, we made it to the sofa and collapsed. My brain was still spinning, pulling memories into my consciousness. Most of my life had been filled with more failures than I could count. Courage was once again slow in coming. My tongue rebelled for fear of another failure. All I could do was hold Margarita's hand and clear my throat. Finally, she came to my rescue. "Tom—you dance better than any of our local caballeros. Where did you learn to dance the flamingo?"

"It was a long time ago. A friend named Jake and a girl named Rosa taught me the steps."

"Where are Jake and Rosa?"

I sure didn't want to tell her that Ma kilt Jake and Rosa was a soiled dove. Those facts would have to wait for another time. "Jake's dead and I lost track of Rosa."

"I'm sorry," she said, squeezing my hand.

Courage finally came while I was looking into her limpid, hazel eyes. "You would love the Bighorn Mountains in Wyoming."

"Is that where you live?"

"Yep, the Sailin' T Ranch."

"You aren't going to join the revolución?"

"Reckon that depends on you."

"On me?"

"Will you come with me to Wyoming?"

Her eyes grew a bit wider as she contemplated my question. "Are you asking me to become your wife?"

Well, there it was. I'd popped the question. The next couple of minutes would either spell success or another failure to join a long list of them. "Reckon I am."

I figured it was a good sign when she didn't answer right away. The better sign was her holding onto my hand as she pondered her answer. "In Méjico, the first thing a man must do is to ask a girls father."

"Okay, if you say so, I will speak with Señor Salinas."

"If he approves, I will go to Wyoming with you."

I embraced her like there would be no other opportunity to do so. "That's the answer I was praying to hear. I will go speak to Señor Salinas tonight."

About that time, my trusty squire tapped me on the shoulder. "Pardon me, compadre, I have good news. You are speaking to General Fabian Fagan, the commander of all the revolución's artillery."

"General?"

"Yes, and General Madero has agreed for you to be my adjutant."

"What's an adjutant?"

"You will be my assistant—Viva Mejico. Viva la revolución, Major Geiger."

I stood up to face my former trusty squire and inform him of my intentions. The Mexican revolution was no concern of mine. "General Fagan, you can inform General Madero that I refuse the appointment."

"My compadre, that will not be wise. Are you forgetting about your share of the silver?"

"Tell Pancho he can keep the silver, compliments of former compañero, Tom Geiger."

Margarita began to sob, jumped up and ran out of the cantina. I tried to catch her, but failed before she entered her father's suite. I rapped on the door and called to her several times, but she didn't answer. Finally, the door opened. A portly lady dressed in a black dress and white apron peered through the doorway. "Señorita Salinas has retired for the evening."

"Por favor," I said, having learned to say please in Spanish. "I must speak with her."

"La mañana," she said, closing the door.

* * *

After spending a sleepless night, I again knocked on the door of Señor Salinas's suite. The same portly maid opened the door.

"Good morning, ma'am. I'm Tom Geiger. Is Señorita Salinas at home?"

She nodded, opened the door wider and gestured for me to follow her. We walked down a hallway and into a sitting room. There, I waited for her to get Margarita. After dawdling with a magazine for several minutes, Señor Salinas walked in and motioned for me to stay seated. "Good morning, Señor Geiger. Might I inquire as to why you wish to speak with my daughter?"

He listened while I told him about everything that had happened in the cantina, including my proposal of marriage and the encounter with Fagan. I didn't wish to remain in Mexico and continue to be involved with their revolution. I had a 25,000-acre ranch to manage in Wyoming. I had become a victim of Fabian Fagan's folly, the absurd idea of breeding camels and llamas to get camellamas. I wished him, Pancho and Madero well in their quest to oust Diaz, but my responsibility was to return to the Sailing T. Finally, I asked for permission to marry Margarita.

"Señor Geiger," he said, stood up and walked over to a window overlooking the patio. He remained silent for several minutes while staring at the garden below. "I understand your need to return to your ranch. Our revolution is the responsibility of Mexicans. We welcome all of the help we can get, but it must be voluntary. As for your share of the silver, it is yours. However, if you wish to contribute part or your entire share to our cause, I would be most pleased. Now, as for your desire to marry my daughter, I have to give you some advice."

Salinas turned from the window and sat down beside me. "Margarita is only nineteen. She has never been alone with a man—always a chaperone has been present. That is our custom. Since Señora Salinas's untimely death this year, I have allowed Margarita to go to the cantina as a hostess only. I hope you understand my meaning?"

"Yes, sir, I never thought she was...."

"A prostitute?"

"No—never."

"Ah, that is good.   Señor Geiger, I believe you are a sincere and honest man. I honor the feelings you have expressed for my daughter. Please do not be offended, but I cannot allow you to speak with Margarita at this time."

"Why?"

"She needs time—time to understand much about these things. I will propose an agreement for you to consider."

"Yes, sir?"

"If you and Margarita have the same affections for each other in one year, you are welcome to return to El Fuerte."

"Okay, but I sure would like to speak to her before I leave."

"It is best that you wait."

It was a difficult solution, but I understood his reasoning. "You may keep my share of the silver, except I need enough money to get back home."

He nodded, pulled out his wallet and handed me a thousand pesos. "I'll tell Margarita about our conversation. Rest assured she will hear the entire story from me. She won't blame you for leaving without seeing her."

The following morning, I met Fagan on the dock at the railroad depot. "Well, General Fagan, I'll look after your camellama until you get back to the Sailing T."

He laughed, pushed up the brim of his Stetson, and then shook my hand. "Aw, Tom, you can keep him."

I thanked him, wished him well and boarded the train. As the locomotive jerked the train into motion, I looked out the doorway, intending to salute my former trusty squire. He was gone, but Señor Salinas and Margarita came running down the loading dock beside the train. She was waving and yelling. "Tom, please wait. Please wait."

As I grasped her hand, Señor Salinas boosted Margarita onto the steps of the car. "El dios va con usted—go with God," he yelled, waving a white handkerchief.

A Sailing T Ranch Feliz Navidad

Christmas Eve came on Wednesday, not quite three weeks after the Japanese pulled their sneak attack on Pearl Harbor. Roosevelt had given his Day of Infamy speech and congress declared war on Hirohito and his backstabbers. We were being pummeled in the first round of World War II. Our forces were undermanned, outsmarted, and being kicked in the butt from Hawaii to the Philippines. It was not a good time to be celebrating Christmas.

A bitter blizzard came sweeping across the mountains before dawn on Christmas Eve morning. It wasn't a good day to crank up our '39 Ford truck and head for Sheridan to pick up Tommy at the railroad depot—but it had to be done. Tommy is our oldest; then there's Rudolph II, named after my pa. Tommy never took to ranching. Pa tried to get him to take over the Geiger Funeral Home in Casper, but he turned it down. Reckon he'd heard me gripe too many times about formaldehyde fumes making my nose run like a dog's with the distemper. It was also against my advice that he decided to become a lawyer, but he did well persuading jurors to see it his way. So, he probably made the right choice. I had disappointed Ma by not studying law and becoming a judge—but she finally found happiness bragging on her grandson to the lady's guild.

Margarita handed me my sheepskin parka, a thermos of hot coffee and a bit of advice. "Take Rudy with you. If you have trouble, he can help."

Rudy had turned out to be kind of a rebel, sort of like me. I wasn't too keen on taking him along. He could be a real pain in the caboose, but she could be right. "Okay, but that will make three of us coming back from Sheridan. It'll be crowded."

She smiled. "Rudy won't take up much room."

Her smiles could always thaw my gizzard and give me that warm feeling, kinda like a shot of brandy after a cold day in the saddle. She was right. Rudy was a tall, gangling teen just as

I was at his age. He'd have to turn around twice to make a shadow. "Get him up, dressed and fed while I fill the radiator with alcohol and hot water."

Rudy was a dawdler, so I had plenty of time to get the Ford ready for the trip. I had the engine running by the time he stepped off the porch and headed for the garage. I could hear him complaining to himself and the Almighty about being rousted out of bed that early. It was bad enough to be driving through blowing snow without listening to a pouting rebel bemoaning his misfortunes.

By the time we had traveled ten miles, the snow was coming down harder. However, the good part was that the wind became less intense. Being grateful for slackened winds was short-lived, as the falling snow became a deluge. Snowflakes, big as quarters, splattered against the windshield and disintegrated into rivulets that refroze within seconds. Right about then, I began to wonder whether we were going to make it to Sheridan before the Ford was done in by the blizzard. The thought of spending Christmas Eve inside one of Henry Ford's contraptions stalled in the middle of a winter storm was disconcerting. It wasn't long before I was forced to stop and clear ice from the windshield by dousing it with alcohol I'd brought along for the radiator.

The heater on a '39 Ford truck had a lot to be desired. Even with it going full blast, the windshield and windows became clouded with freezing condensation. Rudy remained sullen, saying little more than asking how much farther it was to Sheridan. "I could use a little help," I finally said. "Keep the frost wiped off the windshield so I can see the road."

I suppose the urgency of my voice caused some alarm for my sulking companion. He pulled the parka's collar away from his face and sat up on the edge of the seat. "What with?"

"Use your kerchief!"

He wasn't too happy about clearing the windshield, but I managed to keep the Ford on the road with his help. After a lot of stops to pour alcohol on the windshield, we drove into Sheridan. It had taken us over two hours to travel twenty miles. When we pulled up in front of the depot, everything looked vacant—no trains—no activity at all. I set the parking brake and left the engine running, fearful it wouldn't start again "Let's go in and see what's goin' on."

The stationmaster, Harvey Scott, was sympathetic to my urgent questioning. He informed me that the train from Denver, Cheyenne and Casper had been cancelled due to the blizzard. There would be no arrivals until tomorrow, Christmas day, and only then if the weather abated. There was no way to let Margarita know the situation. Ma Bell still hadn't established telephone service in remote areas of Wyoming. So, there was no other choice but to get a room at the Sheridan Inn, deal with a sullen teen and pray for the blizzard to end.

*   *   *

Christmas morning dawned with the storm still venting its fury. At least a foot of powder snow had accumulated and it was still coming down. The only response I got from Rudy when I shook his shoulder to awaken him was a couple of grunts. So, I went to the dinning room to eat breakfast. After enjoying a steaming bowl of oatmeal, I decided to get an update from Harvey Scott. As I walked up to the ticket window, Harvey was penciling an entry into his log. "Excuse me," I said, trying to get his attention.

He continued to write after glancing at me. "I'll be with you in a minute."

"Just wondered whether the train from Casper would be arriving any time soon?"

Harvey closed the log, leaned back in his chair and pointed at the arrival and departure blackboard. "It's all right there."

DELAYED was chalked in the arrival slot beside Cheyenne, Douglas and Casper. "Any idea when it'll get here?"

"Nope."

"Has it left Casper, yet?"

"Don't know."

"Well—y'know where it is now?"

"Nope. It got as far as Douglas last night."

"Well, has it left Douglas?"

"Don't know—the telegraph line went dead."

Ol' Harvey was in a foul mood. No doubt, he was riled about having to work on Christmas day. "What time did they get to Douglas?" I asked, trying to speak in a pleasant manner. It didn't work—my question got to him even more.

He stood up, walked to the window, put his palms on the counter and got his face right up close to mine. "Now, Mister Geiger, I don't know where that train is. It's probably still sittin' in Douglas. The last report I got was that the blizzard was a lot worse between here and Cheyenne. There's a lot of snow on the tracks, so even if they get out of Douglas, it'll take 'em a while to bust through all the snowdrifts between there and here."

I said nothing, just nodded and walked back to the Inn. It was obvious that there would be no train bringing Tommy today. If we didn't want to spend Christmas in a hotel room, I had better get the truck ready and head for the Sailing T.

* * *

The road was in reasonably good condition with no deep drifts with which to contend. Snow fences along the road had kept the drifting to a minimum. Rudy was in a much better mood, which was a welcome change. He even joined me in singing a carol or two. When we were about halfway home, the snowing ceased. It seemed that our luck had changed, a welcome turn during our trek to and from Sheridan.

I should have known our good fortune was going to be short. Wyoming weather can be fickle. When we were about a mile from home, a sudden gale from the west began to sweep powdery snow into billowing clouds. Within minutes, we were enveloped by a swirling ground blizzard. I had to slow the truck down to a creeping pace just to stay on the road. That is when my decision-making came into question. "We should have stayed in Sheridan," Rudy said, turning the heater up to full blast.

There was no disagreement on that comment. Ground blizzards are especially treacherous. Powdery snow crystals are minute, easily stirred into an icy cyclone by gale-force winds. It can strangle the life out of an engine by suffocating the air intake and shorting out the ignition system. Being stranded in a ground blizzard can be lethal. Rudy knew what we were facing. The previous winter had claimed a neighbor when he had died only a few yards from shelter during a ground blizzard. I tried to assure Rudy that we would be home soon, but he just looked at me and shook his head.

We didn't get much farther before the engine sputtered and died. I got out, raised the hood and tried to clean encrusted ice from the air intake. Then, I opened the distributor and attempted to remove ice that was fouling the ignition. My efforts were of no avail. The engine remained dead, not even firing once. Our only refuge was the cab of a lifeless '39 Ford truck—not a pleasant place to be with the wind howling, powdery snow sifting around the doors and the temperature dropping by the minute.

Time crept by, making our torture even more maddening. We were unable to see anything but white, no shapes, no contrasts, just a monotonous canopy of blowing snow. Cold emanated from the windows and floorboard, penetrating our parkas, shoes and gloves. Within the hour, I became convinced that we would not be alive in 24 hours. I glanced at Rudy and saw him shivering and hugging himself. I embraced him and pulled his shaking body close to me. There we sat, hugging one another, hoping and praying for the winds to slacken enough for us to escape our igloo of impending doom.

I kept talking to Rudy, trying to keep him awake. The fear of yielding to sleep kept my tongue busy, talking about anything that came to mind. I wanted Rudy to know more about his Grandfather Salinas. He had no recollections of him. The last time Margarita's father had visited us was only a couple of months after Rudy was born. I told him how I met his mother during my sojourn into Mexico with Fabian Fagan. Ten years after she and I returned to Wyoming and married, his Grandpa Salinas barely escaped execution by forces of President Carranza in January of 1920. He managed to escape from Mexico to Tucson, Arizona, leaving behind his beloved hotel, Posada del Lujo, and most of his fortune. He became an American citizen and was appointed ambassador to Mexico in 1933 and then to the Philippines in 1938 by President Roosevelt. We didn't know what had happened to him since the Japanese attacked and invaded the Philippines right after bombing Pearl Harbor. On and on I rambled—most of what I said, Rudy probably hadn't heard. Each time he seemed to drift into sleep, I gave him a brisk shake. "Stay awake, Rudy. If we sleep, we'll be unaware of dying from the cold."

I had a wealth of experiences to relate, so I began telling him about growing up in Lander and Casper. My experiences with Butch Slade, Doc Ruby, Jake Tillie, Sam Grace, Marshal Tigman, Buffalo Bill and Bill Pickett kept me busy for several hours. During my telling him about solving the murder of Count Rudolph Jäger, sleep finally silenced my tongue. However, I kept right on talking in the dream world to which I had descended.

Someone trying to open the door awakened me. I could see only a shadowy figure because the windows were frosted over from frozen condensation. Then I heard Margarita's voice. "Tom! Rudy! Open the door!"

I tried to move, but my arms were stiff, still embracing Rudy. I managed to pull the door handle and slam my shoulder against the door. It took several lunges before the frozen latch let go. When the door flew open, I fell out into the snow. As I lay there, gazing at the sky that was now clear, no roiling snow, no wind, no clouds, I realized our ordeal was over. Hands began to slap my cheeks to get my attention. Was it an angel? Had I succumbed to the blizzard? Was Rudy alive? All of these questions came to mind as my noggin began to clear. "Tom— can you help me get Rudy out of the truck?"

With a great deal of effort, I manage to stand up and climb back into the truck. It required several vigorous jostles to get Rudy awake. "Wake up, son. The storm's over."

"Feliz Navidad, Momma, " he said, looking past me.

"Feliz Navidad, Rudy," Margarita said, reaching for Rudy's hand.

All three of us climbed on our John Deere tractor and headed for home. When I asked Margarita how she happened to come looking for us, she said I wouldn't understand.

"Sure I will—why did you crank up the tractor and head toward Sheridan to find us? We could have been stalled 15 miles away, or maybe have been in a warm room at the Sheridan Inn?"

"I heard you telling Rudy to stay awake."

"You what…?"

"Over and over, I heard you say, "Stay awake, Rudy. Stay awake, Rudy."

I had no reason to question what she had experienced. There are many things in this world that are enigmas to us. "Thank God you heard me. Feliz Navidad, Margarita—Rudy— Merry Christmas.

Headin' For The Last Roundup

I was reading a readiness critique from the 90th Strategic Missile Wing Headquarters when the intercom light glowed red. The familiar voice of Staff Sergeant Jakes informed me that my brother, Judge Thomas A. Geiger, wished to speak with me on the phone. I laid the critique aside and picked up the handset. "Hello, Tom—what's up?"

"Rudy, I just got a disturbing call from Sheriff Stone up at Sheridan."

"What did he say?"

"Pop's missing."

"Missing?"

"He rode into the mountains to hunt elk three days ago."

"Alone?"

"Yeah."

"He's 85—too old to go alone."

"You know Pop."

"Reckon I do."

"Sheriff Stone is organizing a search-party at the ranch in the morning. He wants us to be there if we can make it."

"Sure," I said, flipping open my Rolodex file. "I'll call Cheyenne Air Services and have our Bonanza serviced and ready by dawn."

After Tom assured me that he would be at the airport by first light, I scanned my duty schedule, phoned Cheyenne Air and called Colonel Hazlet to secure an emergency leave.

When Mom died two years before from cancer, Pop really took it hard. He'd lost his soul mate—that's for sure. He moped around the house, but would occasionally saddle his black and white Paint to ride out and check the cattle. He rarely visited any of the neighbors or drove the pickup into Sheridan like he used to do. We had been concerned, but he always replied in an offhanded manner—"Don't y'be worryin' 'bout me. I'm fine."

It was unusual for Pop to hunt elk and deer by himself. He wasn't a loner, preferring the company and camaraderie of hunting companions. Unless an elk had been bagged late in the day, he seldom would stay out overnight. The temperature can fall below zero in high country during November, which could be disastrous for an 85-year-old man. The more I pondered, the greater my concern grew for what we might find tomorrow.

* * *

As the inky eastern sky began to pale the following morning, I walked out of the Cheyenne Air Terminal and headed for a row of drab, corrugated-steel "T" hangers. It was cold. A thin mantle of frost covered the tarmac and several planes tied down next to the terminal. I glanced skyward and pulled the fleecy collar of my parka up around my neck and chin. The morning star was hovering in a cloudless sky just above the horizon. A light northwesterly breeze, unusual for Cheyenne any time of year, nettled my face like a splash of aftershave. The weather center had assured me our flight would be clear with unlimited visibility all the way to Sheridan. The only minus was the forecast of moderate headwinds above 1,200 feet.

A familiar voice called, "Colonel Geiger," as I walked by the Cheyenne Air office. Jim Horner, the night manager, pulled on his parka as he came to meet me.

"Yeah, Jim—y'got the plane ready?"

"Sure do. I've had the heater bonnet around the cowl for over an hour. She should be warmed up and raring t'go."

"Thanks—have you seen Judge Geiger?"

"Yup, he's waitin' in the hangar."

"Let's roll her out," I said, heading for the hangar.

"Well—it's about time," Tom said as we slid the hangar doors open. "Except for checkin' the oil, I've completed the preflight."

That was a characteristic of Tom. He was always a take-charge type—anything needing to be done was taken care of without delay. He always treated me as if I were a son instead of his brother. I suppose that was because he was six years older, and I was his awkward sibling that needed protection and guidance. While I inherited Pop's blue eyes and lean build, Tom was more robust like our Grandpa Salinas. He also had Mom's hazel eyes and dark complexion. Even though he never wanted to be a rancher, Stetson hats, Justin cowboy boots, and fringed suede-leather jackets were his usual attire. The only other garments hanging in his chambers' closet were the black judicial robes he wore during court sessions.

"Thanks, Tom, I filed our flight plan and the weather is CAVU all the way."

Tom motioned for me to follow him. "Okay, while Jim shuts down the heater and checks the oil, we need to talk."

Once outside of the hangar, he unbuckled his valise, pulled out a file and handed it to me. "I'll do the flyin' while you read these papers. I figure it's time you knew all of the facts."

* * *

We were airborne in our new, blue and white '65 Bonanza and headed for the Sailing T Ranch just as the sun began to rim the eastern horizon. I was reminded of the 90th Strategic Missile Wing's mission as we avoided restricted no-fly zones guarding Minute Man silos that were scattered between Cheyenne and Wheatland. Any missile hidden inside one of those silos could eradicate Moscow from the face of the earth. The thought was both comforting and disconcerting. We were all aware of the fragile restraints that might be pushed aside at any moment, catapulting us into a war that would annihilate mankind. World War II and the Korean War had certainly touched our family. A guard in a Japanese prison camp had killed Mom's father after the fall of the Philippines. Also, Tom had been a naval aviator. He took flight training at Pensacola, Florida and was later assigned to the Yorktown as a Dauntless dive-bomber pilot. After the Yorktown was sunk during the Battle of Midway in June of '42, he transferred to fighters. He flew Grumman F4F Wildcats off of several carriers, the last being the Enterprise during the Naval Battle of Santa Cruz. I graduated from West Point in '50, was commissioned in the Air Force and completed combat pilot training at Nellis Air Force Base in Nevada. I then flew a number of missions in a F-86 Saber over Korea before the cease-fire in '53.

I transferred to missiles in '56 and received an advanced degree in missilery and aeroballistics from M.I.T. in '60. When I was assigned to Francis E. Warren Air Force Base in '64, Tom and I decided to buy a Beechcraft Bonanza. It was an easy decision. We lived in Cheyenne, Wyoming and both loved to fly. Tom had most of the money needed to finance a new plane, having made his fortune investing in Gas Hills uranium mines. He could have retired but the law and being a United States Circuit Court judge for the District of Wyoming was in his blood. If Grandma Geiger were still alive, she would be touting her grandson, the honorable Judge Thomas A. Geiger, to the Casper Ladies Guild.

*　*　*

Tom avoided mountain turbulence by veering east of the Laramie and Bighorn mountains. While he was busy flying, I became lost in thought, almost hypnotized by the steady drone of the engine. The air was exceptionally smooth, uncharacteristic of Wyoming. I pondered Pop's rather careless sojourn into the mountains, pushing his luck to its maximum—foolishness in every aspect for an 85-year-old man. Was he really that reckless, or could there be another reason for his brash behavior? The question was bouncing around in my mind when Tom tapped my knee. "Better get t'readin' those papers—there's a lot in there for you to learn."

I nodded, unfastened the envelope and pulled out a dossier about a quarter inch thick. The pages were bound with a clasp used by lawyers to secure the leaves of a brief. The cover page held a single statement written in Pop's handwriting: *ARCHEOLOGY OF THE MEDICINE WHEEL—THOMAS GEIGER, SR. AND JOHNNY TWO FINGERS.* I turned to the next page and saw that it was also handwritten on lined paper with pen and ink. In fact, the entire dossier was composed in the same manner. I returned to the second page and began to read. *To: Thomas A. Geiger, Jr. From: Thomas Geiger, Sr. The following records are all of those compiled by Johnny Two Fingers and me during our excavation of The Medicine Wheel. It is an ancient stone shrine built by some forgotten tribe on the crest of Medicine Mountain. It contains 28 spokes, a central cairn, five sighting cairns, and has a circumference of 245 feet. According to Johnny Two Fingers great grandfather, Crow Chief Plenty Coups, it was built before the arrival of the people who had no iron. I am sending you these records for two reasons: 1. I am 85 years old, having outlived my parents and grandparents by 10 years. So, reckon I'm about ready to head for the last roundup. 2. Johnny Two Fingers, is even older than I am. We both want this information passed on to the appropriate folks in order that the Crow, Cheyenne and Lakota Indians are properly reimbursed for the wrongs committed by the United States government.*

I continued to read what Pop had written for the rest of our flight to the Sailing T. It was quite interesting and a bit unbelievable. Time passed at an accelerated pace and suddenly we were circling the airstrip Pop had built east of the ranch compound. Pop's foreman, Clay Stuart, had used the strip and a Piper Super Cub during the previous five years to keep track of their cattle and horses.

Sheriff Stone walked from the ranch house to meet us while Tom and I secured the plane. As I watched him, I was reminded of the intent strides carrying the commanding presence of John Wayne as he challenged outlaws in Howard Hawk's Rio Bravo. Stone, like Wayne's character, Sheriff John T. Chance, appeared to be the embodiment of a frontier lawman. As he approached, discriminating gray eyes, almost hidden beneath the brim of his brown stockman's Stetson, peered first at Tom and then me. I was unable to discern whether or not he was smiling, because a drooping, salt and pepper mustache obscured his lips. A dimpled chin jutting from his square jaw like the cowcatcher of a locomotive conveyed a persona of strength "Howdy, Judge Geiger," he said, sliding his hand along the wing. "This is some bird y'boys are flyin'."

"Good morning, Henry," Tom said. "I'd like for you to meet my little brother, Lieutenant Colonel Rudolph Geiger."

I winced—Rudolph sounded like a pompous moniker. "Howdy, Sheriff—just call me Rudy."

"Sure, Rudy—I'm Hank—Hank Stone."

"Pleased to meet you, Hank. Any news about Pop?"

"Maybe—Clay Stuart spent several hours flying over the Bighorns clear down to Cloud Peak yesterday. He thinks he saw smoke on Granite Pass, but it was too late for him to check any closer."

Tom pulled our luggage out of the baggage compartment and unzipped his briefcase. "I've got a geodetic map showing the topography of the Bighorns. Maybe Clay can show us where he saw the smoke."

"Reckon he can," Hank said. "Let's walk over to the house and ask him."

*   *   *

While Tom and Clay were going over the maps and discussing the smoke sighted the previous evening, Hank and his deputy, Chuck Hall, briefed me on the situation. Clay had sighted a trophy bull ranging in a herd of elk several times during the summer while flying over the headwaters of the Tongue River. Pop was determined to hunt the area soon as the season opened after Clay told him about the bull elk. It would be a 30-mile ride through rugged country—one that could require two days. The morning was clear when Pop rode out to hunt for the elk. No severe weather was in the forecast, so Clay wasn't too concerned when Pop failed to ride in the next day. He had the usual gear loaded on his pack mule: a sack of oats, sleeping bag, camping gear, coffee, jerky, dried fruit, bacon, canned beans and a couple of water canteens. These provisions would be plenty for two days and nights, but his failure to arrive the third day was cause for concern.

Tom and Clay took off within the hour in the Super Cub to fly over Granite Pass where the smoke was sighted. I hitched Pop's horse trailer to his pickup, then saddled and loaded a buckskin gelding. Since I had only read the first part of Pop's dossier, I slipped it into my saddlebags. I had a hunch it might reveal some answers as to the reason for his disappearance. While I was loading enough provisions for several days in the high country, Sheriff Stone walked from the house. "Tom just called on the radio. They flew several low recons over Granite Pass and didn't sight anything out of the way."

"Nothing?"

"No—the pass is snow-covered—no horse, smoke nor tracks."

If Pop had built the fire Clay sighted yesterday, he most likely wasn't there today. If able, he would have made some effort to reveal his presence while the Super Cub was flying over the pass. Then the dossier came to mind. He and Johnny Two Fingers had spent a lot of time at the Medicine Wheel during the previous two years since Mom had died. "I've got a hunch. Let's forget about Granite Pass and head for the Medicine Wheel."

Hank glanced up at the snowcapped Bighorn peaks to the west and shook his head. "The Medicine Wheel? That's close to 50 miles as the crow flies over some rugged mountains. I think we need to check out Granite Pass first. If your father was sick or injured, his horse and mule could have run off."

"I just don't think we'll find him there. He would have signaled Tom and Clay."

"Not if he were incapacitated or...."

Hank's unfinished comment was troubling, one that I didn't want to consider. But, of course, he was right. We did have to search that area because of the smoke sighting by Clay. It was the best and only indication of someone's presence on the pass—hopefully, it was a fire Pop had built. "Okay, why don't you and Chuck drive up to Granite Pass and I'll head for the Medicine Wheel."

"Okay," Hank said, handing me a handheld high-frequency radio. "It might save some time. We need to stay in touch."

"Sure, are you loaded and ready to go?"

He nodded and pulled a pouch of Red Man chewing tobacco from his parka pocket. "Yup, Chuck's loadin' our horses right now. Want a chaw?"

"No thanks—don't use it."

"Too bad. More for me," he said, stuffing a sizable wad into his mouth. "Give me a call on the radio soon as you reach Medicine Mountain."

* * *

I turned the pickup onto Highway 14 at Dayton and headed west up a steep and winding blacktop road. Pop's pickup was a vintage '55 Ford that had received more than its share of dents and scrapes. I glanced in the rearview mirror at a cloud of blue smoke rolling up in front of the trailer. I hoped the pickup wouldn't run out of oil nor would the buckskin get asphyxiated before I got to Medicine Mountain.

As I rounded a curve, the snowcapped pinnacle of Cloud Peak appeared above forested mountainsides to the south. The sight steeped my thoughts with memories of times when Pop and I were hunting for elk in these mountains. I wondered why he would ride out alone since he enjoyed the hunt more than bagging an elk. He liked being with hunting companions—eatin' camp cookin' and tellin' lies, as he would say. Had he decided to go hunting with Johnny Two Fingers?

I met Two Fingers once when I was home on leave following the Korean ceasefire in '53. He was a quiet man who spoke often of his ancestors, the Mountain Crow. They lived and hunted in the Bighorn and Absaroka mountains until the government set aside a reservation for them in southern Montana. He was tall, about six-two, and rather linear in build, sort of like Pop and me. His face had been scarred by the white man's plague, smallpox. He wore a combination of Indian and non-Indian attire—a black "sugarloaf" Stetson, fringed buckskin shirt, black woolen trousers and beaded moccasins. A leather pouch containing medicine fetishes dangled from a leather thong tied around his neck.

One story he loved to tell was about his great grandfather, Plenty Coups, who experienced a prophetic vision when he was a lad of only nine years. It happened soon after the Lakota killed Plenty Coups' brother. He climbed to the top of South Twin Butte in the Little Rockies. There, he fasted and prepared for a vision that would come to any worthy Crow. As promised by the Medicine Fathers, a vision came during the night. An assemblage of ancient warriors informed Plenty Coups that he would become chief of his tribe. In another vision, it was revealed to him that a white tribe would arrive, bringing a new way of life for his people—one that was destined to end the old ways. They would ultimately live in square lodges and till the soil instead of hunting for food. Unfortunately for the Crow, this prophetic vision came to pass.

While pondering about Two Fingers, I recalled another vision he claimed Plenty Coups had experienced. At the time, I wasn't too interested in his story, but now it was beginning to make sense. According to the vision, a stone tablet inscribed with the alphabet of an ancient tribe who built the Medicine Wheel was sealed in the base of the central stone cairn. Other tablets documenting the wheel's function and identity of its builders were sealed in the five sighting cairns.

At that time, I became convinced Pop wasn't, nor had he been stalking an elk on Granite Pass. He and Johnny Two Fingers were at the Medicine Wheel. When I reached Burgess Junction, I took the right fork, Alternate 14, toward the Medicine Wheel atop 10,000-foot Medicine Mountain.

Yellow leaves being stripped from aspens by a brisk breeze fluttered and flitted across the road like butterflies on a warm summer day. The sight rekindled my desire to ride these mountains and stalk a wily elk one more time with Pop. The likelihood of that never happening again caused me to reflect on the times we had hunted together in the high country. Autumn in the Bighorns is a special season, filled with sights, sounds and aromas of nature's preparation for the coming of winter. Groves of quaking aspens growing among evergreen conifers take on a mantle of yellow, which turns the mountainsides into a patchwork of yellow and green. The air is resplendent with aromas of pine and spruce—the bleeping calls of blue grouse— the eerie, high-pitched whistles of a bull elk bugling in the distance—the creaking of saddle leather. How I longed to see Pop astraddle his Paint, leading the way up a mountain incline, his lean torso shifting in the saddle as if he and his horse were one. Around the campfire after a long day in the saddle, the evening was filled with his constant chatter. He loved telling stories about growing up in Lander and Casper. My favorites were about his getting acquainted with Pancho Villa, Buffalo Bill, Teddy Roosevelt and Bill Pickett.

I reached a turnout on Medicine Mountain at about eleven, parked the pickup and trailer and unloaded the buckskin. There was still over a mile of tough terrain to cover before reaching the Medicine Wheel. Sheriff Stone and his deputy should have reached Granite Pass and might have some news about their search for Pop. I pressed the transmit button on the handheld radio. "Hank—this is Rudy—come in."

Only a steady hiss of static was emitted by the radio. Several more attempts to reach them also failed. I stuffed the radio into my pocket, stepped in my stirrup and reined the buckskin up the trail leading to the Wheel. Gusting winds began to rustle the pines and spruce. Dark clouds were rolling across the jagged mountaintops. Soon, the sun was hidden by a turbulent overcast, a portent of an approaching blizzard. The high country during November, called the Moon of Falling Leaves by the Lakota, can experience an abrupt change in the weather. When an arctic front charges over the mountains, a pleasant day can become frigid as the cockpit of a highflying jet. The sudden weather change goaded me into picking up the pace. I snapped the reins and nudged the buckskin with my heels. "Hah, get up, let's find Pop."

The buckskin began to trot, but soon slowed to a steady pace as the incline grew steeper. The trail was a primitive course hewn into the mountain by horse's hooves and a large number of travois over many centuries of time. Crow, Cheyenne, Black Foot, Arapaho and Lakota, had made pilgrimages to the Wheel until the U.S. Army sequestered them on reservations. After a half-mile, the trail forked. I chose the right fork since it appeared to have been more heavily traveled over the years. I reached the tree line around eleven-thirty where the going became more arduous as a frigid gale endeavored to shove the buckskin and me off the windswept summit. I pulled down the brim of my Stetson and shielded my face from the icy blast with the collar of my parka. When we reached the plateau atop the mountain, the stone cairns of the Medicine Wheel came into view. There wasn't a horse or pack mule, or Pop, nothing except stones that had been stacked by an unknown tribe of America's first inhabitants.

I stepped out of my stirrup and tied the buckskin's reins to one of the sighting cairns. Disappointment and frustration swept over me like the winds that were pummeling the mountain crest. Where was Pop? Had he been here during the past three days? While the buckskin turned his rump into the wind to ease nature's onslaught, I searched the Wheel, hoping to discover anything that would confirm my hunch.

The search yielded nothing that would reveal whether anyone had been there during the past several days. I pulled out the radio. "Hank—Sheriff Stone—this is Rudy."

I released the transmit button. This time, the radio came to life. "Hank here—go ahead Rudy."

"Pop's not at the Medicine Wheel. Have you found anything?"

"We found a burned out firepit but nothing else, yet."

"How about Tom and Clay?"

"No positive sightings. They're back at the ranch to refuel before flying up to Medicine Mountain."

"Tell them not to fly up here. The weather is deteriorating. Too much wind and the ceiling is droppin' fast."

"Okay—I'll call 'em. What are you goin' to do now?"

My gut still told me that Pop was somewhere on Medicine Mountain. "Don't know. I'm goin' to cover this area before headin' back to the ranch."

"Okay—give us a call if you find anything."

Pop's dossier came to mind again. Maybe an answer would be somewhere in it. I reined the buckskin back down the trail toward the pickup. Once there, I'd finish reading what Pop had to say about the Medicine Wheel.

*　*　*

I climbed into the pickup after loading the buckskin into the trailer. The fuel gage showed three-quarters of a tank, plenty for running the engine to heat the cab. I started the engine, turned on the heater, opened the dossier and began to read where I had left off on page three.

Two Fingers convinced Pop that Chief Plenty Coups vision was true. The first tribe of humans to occupy North America had built the Medicine Wheel. Its purpose was an enigma, one begging to be solved. Pop had always been bent upon making his mark in the world. Discovering who the wheel-builders were and the reason for its construction became an obsession for him and Two Fingers. It took them two years to arrive at their conclusion.

Pop ordered two sets of astronomy and archeology books after discovering a stone tablet in the central cairn. Contrary to Plenty Coups' vision, which placed the tablet in the base of the cairn, they found it five layers from the top on the north side of the stone pillar. They spent several weeks trying to decipher the inscriptions carved into its surface. Being unable to solve the puzzle, Pop made a charcoal rubbing of the tablet and sent it to Doctor Norman Peters at Cambridge University. Peters, a professor of ancient languages and hieroglyphics, replied in an enthusiastic letter that the inscriptions were of the utmost importance. The builders called themselves, Tama-Kosan, the People of Light. Peters had sent the interpretations to British astronomer Arthur Simpson who was doing research on Stonehenge in the south of England. He compiled astronomical computations and concluded that, like Stonehenge, the Medicine Wheel was a solar-lunar and stellar analog computer. He, also, affirmed there were five additional tablets located in the five sighting cairns located at the periphery of the wheel.

This verification spurred Pop and Two Fingers to search the sighting cairns for the tablets. They were successful and rubbings of their inscriptions were sent to Peters and Simpson. Another enthusiastic letter from Peters and Simpson confirmed their original theory that the wheel was an ancient stellar computer. The five sighting cairns were used to calculate Sun, planet and other star locations. In doing so, the Tama-Kosan, were able to devise a calendar and determine when to migrate from one locale to another. Also, Doctor Peters claimed the Tama-Kosan religious celebrations required their knowing when summer and winter solstices occurred. The wheel is sacred, its existence a testimony to the Tama-Kosan's knowledge of astronomy and knowing how the Sun, planets and stars affected their lives.

Pop's conclusion was that the Medicine Wheel was a national treasure. It must be preserved like any religious relic or archeological discovery. It should not be desecrated or pilfered by non-native Americans. The site should be returned to the Plains Indians so they can continue their religious practices atop Medicine Mountain without interference from the U. S. Government.

With mixed emotions, I slipped the dossier back into the file. Pop had finally achieved something he had desired all of his life—an element of success and recognition. Maybe fame would be his lot after all. But, I was disappointed. There still was no explanation about his disappearance. Maybe he had gone hunting for the elk on Granite Pass. I glanced at my watch. It was ten minutes past one.

I decided to give the sheriff another call on the radio. I was ready to head back to the ranch if he or Tom had discovered anything indicating Pop's whereabouts. "Hank—this is Rudy."

"Yeah, Rudy, did you find anything?"

"No. How abut you or Tom?"

"No, nothing. We're about ready to load the horses and head back to the ranch."

"What about Tom?"

"Y'mean he hasn't flown over Medicine Mountain, yet?"

"No. Didn't you tell him about the weather?"

"I did, but he refused to take your advice. They should have gotten there by now."

After signing off, I shut down the engine. It had begun to snow. The windshield and windows had to be cleaned of ice and snow before driving back to the ranch.

While I cleared ice and snow from the windshield, dejection, frustration and concern filled my thoughts. I recalled the time Pop and I were caught in a ground blizzard during our trek to Sheridan one Christmas Eve. Winter storms can be lethal. The sky was growing darker—the cloud ceiling dropping by the minute. Just as I got back into the pickup and reached for the switch, the familiar drone of an airplane engine stayed my hand. I jumped out of the pickup. Pop's yellow and black Super

Cub came flying about 50 feet above the highway. *My God, it's Tom and Clay.* Just as I waved at them, a message cylinder with a streamer dropped from the plane. Tom's know-how of low level bombing as a navy pilot pinpointed the pickup with nearly perfect accuracy. The cylinder plunged into the snow about 20 yards in front of the pickup. I opened the cylinder and pulled out a sheet of paper. The message was short and to the point: *Our radio is out. We sighted a cave and smoke in a grove of aspens on the north side of Medicine Mountain. I'm sure Johnny Two Fingers ran out of the cave and waved. Check it out! Tom*

I unloaded the buckskin, swung into the saddle and headed up the trail toward the Wheel. Sleet and snowflakes began to sting my face as a howling gale propelled the blizzard across Medicine Mountain. Time was running out. If Pop were still alive, he would have to be found before nightfall. It would not take long for drifting snow to block the highway. It could be hours or even days before the sky cleared, but the temperature would plunge to subzero levels whenever that happened.

Concern for Tom and Clay flying up here under such hazardous conditions urged me to get to the north side of the mountain as quickly as possible. Tom would not leave the area until I found out about Two Fingers and the cave.

Where the trail forked, I followed the left, lesser-traveled fork. It stayed within the forested area, which shielded me from the gale that was flogging the treetops. The buckskin covered another half-mile before a grove of aspen came into view. Sure enough, there was the opening to a cave in the face of a cliff. "Hello—Pop—Johnny," I yelled, kicking the buckskin with my heels. The familiar figure of Two Fingers emerged from the cave. He waved his hat and walked down the incline to meet me. "Hau, Rudy."

I stepped out of my stirrup and grasped Johnny's hand. "Damn, I happy to see you. Have you seen Pop?"

"Him up there in Cave of Warriors," he said, pointing at the cliff.

"Thank, God. If it hadn't been for Tom and you, I nor anyone else would have found Pop before the spring thaw."

"Johnny grimaced and pointed at the low overcast. "White goose of the north flapping wings—big wind—big snow."

"Yeah, I know Johnny. How's Pop?"

"Come—you see."

"Where are Pop's Paint and pack mule?" I asked as we walked toward the cave.

"He give my grandson, Little Tall Man."

"He gave them to your grandson—why did he do that?"

"Your Pop like Little Tall Man. No need pony and mule."

That was a puzzling statement. Pop loved that Paint. He wouldn't up and give him away. Maybe he would the mule, but not his favorite pony. "Why?"

Two Fingers ignored my question. *He and Pop must have some kind of deal*, I thought, so the issue was dropped.

I tied the buckskin to an aspen in front of the cave. Johnny lit a kerosene lantern and led the way down a corridor into a room of sizable proportions. In the center was a firepit of smoldering alder logs. Smoke from the fire exited through a natural vent shaft in the ceiling. I looked around for Pop, but could see nobody in the flickering lantern light. "Where's Pop?"

"Him there," Johnny said, gesturing toward a dark corner of the room.

"Hi, Pop," I said, trying to see him.

"Him no talk," Johnny said. "Spirit fly with eagles."

Knowing his meaning, I knelt beside the silent form wrapped in deerskin.

"Oh—Pop. Why?"

Johnny Two Fingers explained what had happened. Pop was aware that he was dying from cancer of the pancreas. He knew there was little time left for him, so he chose how he wished to join Mom in the hereafter. When he sensed the time was near, the trophy elk was a good excuse to saddle up and ride out on a supposed hunting venture. He'd had his fill of digging graves and the eye-smarting effects of formaldehyde while growing up in Casper. If he had anything to do with it, nobody was going to fill his veins with such noxious stuff. He wanted to be wrapped in a deerskin creosoted by pine smoke and suspended on a Mountain Crow burial scaffold. Finally, Johnny told me that Pop's dying wish was for the Medicine Wheel to be set aside as a national monument. All of the information relative to the building and reasons for its creation were contained in the dossier he had sent to Tom Jr.

After listening to Johnny Two Fingers explanation, I walked out of the cave and called the sheriff. "Hank—this is Rudy—come in."

The radio came to life. "Yeah, Rudy. Where are you?"

"I'm on Medicine Mountain at the Cave of Warriors."

"You're where?"

"I found Pop. He's in the Cave of Warriors."

"How is he?"

"Just fine. He's flying with the eagles."

About that time, the yellow and black Super Cub did a low level flyover. I pulled off my scarf and waved it back and forth. The plane wagged its wings, rolled into a sharp banking turn and headed east toward the Sailing T.